A CREEL OF IRISH STORIES

"Οσσ' ἕλομεν, λιπόμεσθ' · ὅσα δ' οὐχ ἕλομεν, φερόμεσθα."

A

Creel of Irish Stories

BY

JANE BARLOW

Short Story Index

Short Story Index Reprint Series

 BOOKS FOR LIBRARIES PRESS
FREEPORT, NEW YORK

First Published 1898
Reprinted 1970

STANDARD BOOK NUMBER:
8369-3436-9

LIBRARY OF CONGRESS CATALOG CARD NUMBER:
70-116934

PRINTED IN THE UNITED STATES OF AMERICA

CONTENTS

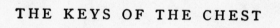

THE KEYS OF THE CHEST

THE KEYS OF THE CHEST

THE little valley of Letterglas is a very green and very lonesome place almost always, for snow seldom lies on it, and the few people who come into it depart again even sooner and as tracelessly, so that its much grass spreads from month to month uncovered and untrodden. It runs westward—that is, towards the ocean—but never reaches the shore, because a great grassy curtain intervenes, curved round the end of it, and prolonged in the lower hill-ranges that bound it to north and south. They are just swarded embankments of most simple construction, with scarcely a fold to complicate the sweep of their smooth green slopes, and the outline of their ridge against the sky undulates as softly as young corn in a drowsy breeze. Only at one point —about midway on the right hand looking westward—it is suddenly broken by a sharp dip down and up again, making a gap like an inverted Gothic arch. And this is called by everybody *the Nick of Time*. I once asked the reason of a gossoon who was guiding me

3

over the opposite hills, but he replied: "Sure, what else would they be callin' it?" Nor have I ever yet lighted upon a more satisfactory explanation.

The effect of Letterglas's solitude and verdure somehow seems to be heightened if one notices its single visible sign of human handiwork. This is a road-track, now all but quite grassed over, leading into the valley from its open end, where the Clonmoragh highway passes, and stopping aimlessly at the slope immediately below the Nick, having first flung two or three zig-zag loops up the hillside. A rust-eaten, handleless shovel, and the wreck of an overturned wheelbarrow, still mark the point where the work was abandoned on a misty morning in April, more than fifty springs ago; but the track itself is now merely a most faint difference of shade in the sward, which has crept back again indefatigably, even where the austere road-metal had been thrown clattering down.

A day before that misty morning, if anybody had climbed up and had passed through the Nick of Time, in at which the new road was to go, he would have found himself on a long level of fine-bladed turf, stretching like a lofty causeway laid down atop of the hill-embankment. Everything else up there looked so softly smooth and flecklessly green that the eye was at once caught by a big block of stone, which stood just opposite the gap, at a few yards' distance. It was an oblong mass of blackish limestone, perhaps seven feet by four, with a shape curiously sym-metrical for a piece of Nature's rough-hewing; plumb-and-rule guided chisel could scarcely have made its lines truer. That, and its solitariness, uncompanioned as far as could be seen by so much as a single pebble, gave its aspect an incongruity which prompted the question how it had come there; for whose answer we must revert through unimaginable wastes of years to the time when our last huge ice-sheet was scoring and grinding all the country's face on its slithering way to the western ocean. Then it was that this big boulder dropped fortuitously through a small rent in the isle-wide coverlid, and so being left behind did not share in the final welter-ing plunge a few miles farther on, where the stark folds slipped over the sea-cliffs like the counterpane off a restless sleeper's bed. Ever since that catastrophe it had sat there looking rather like a rude unwieldy coffer or chest, a portion—as in fact it had been—of the impedimenta carried and lost by some Titanic traveller. The resemblance was increased by a clean-cut horizontal crack, no doubt sustained when the mass came *sogging* heavily to earth, which ran all round it, a few inches from the top, counterfeiting a lid. All the old ages that had passed over it afterwards had wrought only slight changes in its aspect. As the years went on, the dark peaty mould deepened a little about its base, and dull golden and silvery lichen-circlets crept out here and there like wraiths of the sun and moon beams that had touched it. Otherwise it was unaltered, and for many a long century so were its surroundings.

But at last a new feature appeared among them; a very inobtrusive one. Fifty years ago, anybody approaching the big stone from the Nick of Time might have observed that a little footpath led up to it from the contrary direction, and went no farther. A more inartificial path could not well be: a simple product of steps going to and fro. You might have supposed a sheep-walk, only that there were no fleeces nibbling over Letterglas.

Indeed, its most frequent passers-by being such promiscuous wayfarers as the shadows of wings and clouds, it was not easy to conjecture any plausible *raison d'être* for this track, which ran distinctly defined, though faintly, merely a crease in the flowing sward mantle, not a seam worn threadbare, so to speak, through to the brown earth. Certainly the rather gloomy-looking block had no apparent attractions wherewith to invite resort, not even a view, as it stood at the bottom of a very shallow dent in the green. Yet there the path ended; and if you took a dozen steps to the brow of the hill, you could trace the course of that pale thin line far down the slopes; through the fenceless " mountainy land " first, and then into two or three steep, dyke-girdled fields, before it was lost among the round-topped trees which gathered about a rambling old mansion-house. Whoever visited the big stone evidently thought it worth while to come a long way.

Such an humble and artless path has always a certain element of romance about it, lacking in more pretentious thoroughfares contracted for at so much a mile. They differ as does a brook from a canal. Like the brook, which has wrought itself as it went along, with and by its own purpose, the little footpath has some special meaning and object, albeit perhaps a less obvious one. It is the visible trail of a want or wish, though of what kind we may be unaware, and with want or wish it will cease to exist, or soon after. For the living green things will creep back and efface it speedily. But meanwhile it seems half to keep and half to betray a secret: you can only guess what has brought feet thither day by day to tread it out.

*   *   *   *   *   *

Fifty years ago or more, you would have been likely enough any fine morning to catch the chief maker of this particular path in the act. If the years were, say, ten more, it would have proved to be a very little little-girl, whose brown hair held both sunshine and shadow, and whose hazel-green eyes were softly lit, and who in those early days of hers always wore an ugly reddish checked pelisse, and a broad-brimmed straw hat with velvet rosettes to match. This was little Eileen Fitzmaurice, six or seven years old, who, ever since she could recollect anything, and maybe some twelve months longer, had lived with her mother and aunt at the Big House in Glendoula. As you would, no doubt, never guess her errand up the side of Slieve Ardgreine, I will at once explain that she was seeing after the safety of her family plate.

Although Eileen had herself no recollection of anywhere else than this Glendoula, a valley much resembling its neighbour Letterglas, but with its green dotted and chequered by a few cabins and fields, she knew by hearsay that there was another place in the world, a most wonderful place called Drumlough Castle or At Home, where "there wouldn't be as much as a wing of a cold chicken served in the parlour without its silver dish under it, and as for the ould black sideboard of an evenin' there would be company in it, that now was somethin' worth lookin' at ; the full moon on a dark night was a joke to the big salvers." To be sure there were there other fine things innumerable, which would have appealed quite as strongly to her imagination, if they had had equal justice done to them ; however, it was upon these that Eileen's informant always laid most stress, for she looked back to her ancient home through the eyes of old Timothy Gabbett, the lame butler, whose pride and affection had dwelt in his pantry and plate - chest, enjoying their supreme moments before a gala-night spectacle of snowy and crystal and lustrous argent gleams.

Yet this paradise, of which old Timothy used to say mournfully, " Ah, Miss Eileen, them was the rael times," was haunted by lurking shadows. Eileen never learned the true reason of their exile : how wild Sir Gerald, her father, had been found one summer morning entangled among the serpentine coils of the water-weeds at the end of the lake, with his only son and heir dead in his arms, three-year-old Jack, who, when told by the garden-boy Mick that the master was looking for him high ways and low ways, had stumped off greatly elated, with no foreboding of the method in which Sir Gerald had resolved to settle his grievously involved affairs. She had been too small a baby then to be conscious of her mother's flight from the memories of Drumlough, and the circumstances of their coming to Glendoula remained for her in their original obscurity. But she very quickly perceived that it was worse than useless to

ask questions on such subjects of anybody
except old Timothy, and that any allusion
to his stories in the presence of her elders
was a grave misdemeanour, which made her
invalid mother cry, and her melancholy aunt
scold; and Eileen would have desisted at a
subtler hint. She did not often wonder why
this should be, because her world was so full
of mysteries that she generally accepted their
existence as a matter of course. There was
just one of them, however, that exercised her
mind not a little, and that she sometimes
vainly tried to get cleared up. She wanted
to know what had become of all those most
beautiful silver things that Timothy talked
about — the great shining salvers, the claret-
jugs, the tankards and flagons, the piles "as
high as your head, Miss Eileen," of plates
with a polish on them "the stars in the sky
might be the better of gettin'," and the
grand potato-rings, and the frosted cake-
baskets, and the tall *up-urny*, which seemed
to be a marvellous composition of lights and
flowers. Of all these resplendent objects, the
only one, a few uninteresting spoons and forks
excepted, that apparently had moved with the
family to Glendoula, was an antique teapot

of fantastic shape. It could no longer be used for its proper purpose, owing to the infirmity of its dragon-tail handle, but old Timothy turned it to account in his own way. You would always have been warned that it was Quality—and Quality was almost invariably either Dr M'Clintock or Canon Roche —who had called at Glendoula House had you seen Timothy hobbling to answer the bell. For, having reconnoitred through the half-glass back-hall door, it was his practice in such cases to equip himself with the old teapot and a bit of "shammy," that he might appear rubbing up ostentatiously, and muttering a stereotyped apology: "Beg your pardon, sir, but there does be such a terrible sight of silver clanin' in this house that I scarce git time to lay a bit out of me hand." All the while he felt more than half-conscious that it was a poor and rather unseemly pretence; but he had not much invention, and could devise no better expedient for the magnifying of his diminished office and the upholding of the family's fallen fortune. Nor was he ready with any very satisfactory answers when Eileen questioned him about the present bestowal of his treasures. Full well he knew that they had long since gone to the Jews and other hopeless destinations, and were by this time irrecognisably melted down, or, more intolerable still, adorning alien boards, and subject to alien powder and brushes. This knowledge gave him acute pangs, which made his replies curt and vague. "Where are they now, Miss Eily? Ah, sure, just put away somewheres safe; they're not wanted these times, when the poor misthress is seein' no company; but it won't be so one of these days. . . Ah no, Miss Eily darlint, I couldn't be showin' them to you—sure, they're not in this house at all." And once he added: "They're just stored up handy, Miss Eily, waitin' till you're grown a big enough lady to be ownin' of them."

"Me?" said Eileen, startled.

"Why, in coorse, Miss Eileen. Who else has anythin' else to say to thim after poor little Master Jack, that had a right to ha' been Sir John, gettin' dhrown—bein' took suddint, I mane, that way? Hiven be good to the both of them. Ay, to be sure, honey, it's all in a very safe place waitin' for you. And thank'ee kindly for bringin' me in the grand little bunch of daisies—they smell iligant."

After learning this fact about her far-off proprietorship in the hoarded plate, Eileen thought about it oftener than ever, though from motives of delicacy she spoke about it seldomer, lest she should appear unduly prying and eager on her own behalf. And for a long time the more she pondered the matter, the less possible she found it to excogitate any possible hiding-place. But at last she made a fateful discovery.

*   *   *   *   *   *

It was one fine May morning when she went for an unusually long ramble with Norah Kinsella, the housemaid. Norah — a tall, strong, cheerful lass, far more active than rheumatic old nurse — thought nothing of carrying her pet, little Miss Eileen, who at six years old was still only "a light fairy of a crathur," up and down steep places, so that they could go all the farther. On this occasion they climbed right up to the top of the hill behind the house, higher than Eileen had ever been before ; and one of the first things she noticed was the great boulder-block. She never had seen a stone of nearly so large a size, nor imagined one ; and she did not now

class it with the small unshapely fragments
and insignificant pebbles with which she was
familiar.   Rather, it reminded her of the turf-
stacks that she had watched people building
up carefully in the yard.   Yet a turf-stack
it certainly was not.

"Doesn't it look like a great big box,
Norah?" she said.

"Ay, indeed does it, Miss Eily," Norah said;
"and a fine power of things it 'ud hould
inside of itself, too.   Sure now, you could
be puttin' away a one of them little houses
down below there in it, or very nearly."

"It must be extrornarly heavy, Norah,"
Eileen said, patting the sun-warmed side of
the stone with her hand.   "If that's its lid,
I couldn't lift it."

"Sorra a bit of you, honey, nor ten like
you.   Troth, 'twould take ten strong men to
give that a heft," said Norah, making as if
she would prise it up with the flat of her
hand.   "Whativer was inside it 'ud have to
stay there for you or for me, if it was silver
or gould itself—we'd ha' ne'er a chance."

Her random words gave Eileen the shock of
a new idea.   Perhaps there really might be
silver, quantities of silver, in it.   For why

should not this be the handy safe place that old Timothy meant? A safer there could not well be, since it was so far removed from all meddlers; and she almost thought that she did espy a bright twinkle as she stared hard at the lid-like crack, which was just on a level with her eyes. She discreetly said nothing about it to Norah, and her pre-occupation with the subject made her so abstractedly silent on their way home that Norah feared the walk must have been too long. But, in fact, she was considering whether or no she should mention her discovery to old Timothy. He might be vexed, she thought, at her finding out what he had refused to tell her: still, she would have liked to ask him whether her guess were right. The point needed much deliberation, and remained undecided for many days.

*   *   *   *   *   *

Meanwhile she chanced upon something that seemed to be an independent corroboration of her own theory. By nature Eileen had not particularly studious tastes, but solitariness had early driven her to seek for company on the shelves in the long low-windowed book-room. She did not find there much that was very congenial.   Sixty years ago juvenile literature was, as a rule, a solemn and dreary thing ; and Eileen's meagre library was not even up to that date, having for the most part belonged to the preceding generation.   The favourite authors of the day would appear to have been infested with a mole-like fancy, which commonly led them to linger among tombs and worms and epitaphs, seldom, indeed, stopping short at those grisly precincts, or forbearing to light them up with a lurid flare from the regions beyond, but, nevertheless, dwelling upon them with a fond elaboration of detail. Accordingly, a few days after her first ascent of Slieve Ardgreine, Eileen fished down from its shelf a small, old dusty, half-calf volume, which was composed of several short stories bound together.   One of them, entitled *The Churchyard Prattler*, related the experiences of a child, aged four, who, as an appropriate and improving pastime, was sent out provided with a string of his own length, and instructed to ascertain by measurement how many of the graves in his cheerfully chosen playground were shorter than himself.   He was pictorially represented as attired in a long bib and a broad - brimmed chimney - pot hat, and he

B

moralised his lively researches into the strains
of a brief rime-doggerel hymn :

> " *Oft may be found*
> *A grassy mound*
> *By the yew-tree,*
> *Much less than me ;*
> *It seems to cry :*
> *Prepare to die !* "

Another showed how a frivolous little girl,
in a huge coal-scuttle bonnet, had her sinful
hankering after toys and such vanities rebuked
by being conducted past a series of attractive
shop-windows, from each of which she was
bidden to select herself a present, until she
arrived at an undertaker's establishment, where
she was likewise required to place an order.

The last story in the volume, however, was
of a very different type, and upon it Eileen
now alighted, instinctively judicious in her
skipping of its ghoulish companions. It was
called *The Glittering Hoard in the Coffer of
Stone*; and the passage that most profoundly
impressed her ran as follows : " The flare of the
scented torches fell upon the vast coffer of
dark stone, which stood in one corner of the
cavern. Its smooth sides were crusted here
and there with patches of lichen and grey
moss, and it looked as if no hand had touched

it for many an age.   But at a gesture from the
Prince, six gigantic black slaves raised up the
massive slab which formed its lid.   As they
did so, the foot of one of them slipped, and
before he could recover himself, the unwieldy
weight slid down with a crash, and was
shattered into three fragments on the floor.
Nobody heeded, however, for the light that
broke out of the open chest drew all eyes
thither.   It was like a cistern filled with
crystalline fire.   "Empty it, my son," said the
old Sultaness, and the Prince began to lift out
one by one the treasures it contained.   Silver
goblets there were and flagons, great gilt bowls
and ewers, filigree caskets set with diamonds,
chains of red gold, and ropes of milk-white
pearls, diadems and necklaces, armlets and
girdles, whose pendant gems dripped a many-
coloured brilliance, as of flower-distained dew.
At the bottom of the chest lay a round golden
buckler, studded with knots of jewels, and a
mighty sword in an ivory scabbard inlaid with
pale coral and amber : the hilt was carved out
of a single lump of apple-green chrysoprase.
All these, strewn over the flagged floor,
shimmered and bickered under the glancing
torch-gleams, until it seemed as if a rippled

and moon-lit sea lay there flashing around a murky rock. The beholder could hardly realise that its uncouth bulk had indeed been the receptacle of a treasure so richly wrought and exquisite."

Eileen read and pored over this account with keen interest and pleasure. From the first she drew a parallel between the two great blocks of stone, so that the wealth disclosed by the one strengthened her most splendid conjectures about the other. As she read, she easily shifted the scene from the shadowy cavern to the sunny hill-top, and imagined the grass all scattered over with shining gear, which by some strange decree of fortune she was to look upon as her own property. Silver dishes and jewelled diadems, the *up-urny* and the buckler, both these alike fascinatingly mysterious, sparkled for her in the clear light of day. The only objects in the picture that she shrank from reproducing were those six gigantic black men, whose presence she felt to be an ugly blot upon the brightness. But then she reflected that the lifters of the lid perhaps need not be either black or gigantic. Dan Donnelly, and Christy Shanahan, and Murtagh Reilly, would surely be strong and big enough to do it; and they were all pleasant familiar faces, who said "Good mornin' to you kindly, Miss Eily," or "The Lord love you," with friendly smiles, whenever they met her, and were in no wise alarming. So she substituted them for the formidable figures, and could almost hear old Murtagh saying, "Hup boyos! or what for was yous aitin' all them pitaties?" which was his usual exordium upon such strenuous occasions.

*　　*　　*　　*　　*　　*

The next time that she went for a walk with Norah Kinsella, which happened soon after this, in the continuance of old nurse's rheumatism, Eileen said, half-scared at her own temerity: "Let us go up again to the big box"; and she felt happy when Norah at once assented, tacitly accepting the fact that a box it was. Eileen wanted to see whether she were tall enough to look in, supposing the lid removed, and she found, to her gratification, that on tiptoe her stature sufficed.

It was some while longer, however, before she ventured to touch upon it in conversation with old Timothy; nor did she then make any point-blank statement. She introduced the subject allusively and implicitly. "That *is* an exceedingly safe place where you keep the plate now, Timothy, isn't it?" she said to him one day when she was helping him to lay the table, by following him with a little sheaf of spoons as he hobbled round it. Her brown frock was hidden beneath a white cambric pinafore, and her large eyes glinted wistfully through a soft cloud of hair.

"It is so bedad, missy," said the old man resignedly, "we've took good care of that."

"How many people do *you* think it would take to lift off the lid of the chest?" said Eileen.

"Is it the led, Miss Eily? Troth, now, they'd be bothered to do that on us at all, if they was as many as they plased, and the kay of it put away out of the raich of them—or the likes of them," old Timothy said, arbitrarily blackening her colourless term.

"Oh, then, it's locked?" said Eileen.

"To be sure it is, Miss Eily. Why now, if it wasn't, you might as well be gad'rin' the things together handy for villins to run away wid thim convanient. But ah, sure, you're innicent yet, Miss Eily, and small blame to you, or you'd understand the raison of kays."

"So I do, Timothy," said Eileen. "It's villins. But I think I don't quite understand the reason of *them*."

She went away pondering. This locking of
the chest compelled her to modify somewhat
the details of the opening scene. However,
she quickly re-arranged them completely to her
satisfaction, and her fondness for visiting the
site of it did not diminish. About this time
she began to be allowed to ramble out un-
attended, for old nurse went invalided home,
and Eileen had acquired the character of a
quiet, sensible child, not apt to get into mischief.
The use she made of her liberty was a daily
pilgrimage up to the big stone, where she
dreamed away many pleasant hours, largely
occupied with plans for the future, when she
should have found that key. Sometimes she
brought the *Glittering Hoard* book up with
her, and read it there to whet the edge of
anticipation; but in general she was content
to weave a dazzling fabric out of the material
supplied her by old Timothy's reminiscences.

Should anybody hence infer that Eileen
Fitzmaurice must have been in her early youth
an avaricious sort of person, he cannot be
flatly contradicted; for so she was, in a way.
But in a way it was. Her theories about the
privileges of property were peculiar, and re-
strictive. For instance, in her definition "my

own" meant merely "promptly transferable";
and the Paradise she supposed was a place
where everybody else would like everything
that she had. Here, the failure of her few
possessions to please other people not infre-
quently caused her disappointment; and she
occasionally thought scorn of herself for having
only trifles to offer so scant and paltry. Sometimes, indeed, it was nothing better than a
bunch or so of blackberries, perhaps wanting
still several shades of their mature glossy jet,
which she had torn hands as well as frock in
extricating from among their barbed briers—
the greediest child never plucked with a more
eager recklessness. When she could meet
with no friend who was imprudent or com-
plaisant enough to accept these spoils, she
would, a little crestfallen and regretful, scatter
them on some walk or window-stool, in hopes
that at least the small birds might condescend
to benefit thereby. She was all the more
dependent upon opportunities for bestowing
such a tangible proof of her regard, because
she seldom had any for others of the less material
kind. Her mother was too drearily isolated
by ill-health and despondency to be within
reach of caresses, while her aunt Geraldine was

mostly absent, inhabiting some remote volume, and seemed to be rather bored by the people whom she encountered in her brief visits to the outer world. The acquisition of the wonderful chest, however, would release Eileen from these straitened circumstances, as its contents would surely comprise what could not but give satisfaction to all. She could scarcely believe that anybody, not even poor mamma, who only pretended so badly to care about her presents of wild flowers and the like, could really be indifferent to the set of six little silver salt-cellars shaped like water-lilies, which old Timothy described so fondly. It might be possible also to provide Aunt Geraldine with something of which she should not say hurriedly, coming reluctantly out of her book: "Oh, thank you, my dear child, but what use would it be to *me*?" Then there were Norah Kinsella, and old nurse, and old Timothy, and after them a small crowd of neighbours, very adequately representing the population of Glendoula, so catholic being Eileen's good will that there was hardly a dresser in the hamlet on which some brilliant object should fail to shine. And if anything remained over after the distribution, she thought to herself that she would leave it for the villins, who would no doubt be much disappointed, supposing they ever did come to look and found nothing at all. Such plans as these were commonly in her mind as she toiled up and trotted down the smooth-swarded steps, where the thread-like track of 'her footsteps slowly began to follow them.

*   *   *   *   *   *

Generally Eileen went to and fro quite alone beneath the spacious domed skies, which seemed to make no more account of her than of the rabbits, who played here and there on the side of the hill. The rabbits evidently did not think much of her either, and hid themselves when she came near without any great show of flurry or fright, rather intimating by their demeanour that they had simply no wish to make her acquaintance. But Eileen used to watch them wistfully from their prescribed distance, and think to herself that they looked enviably sociable and friendly together. Sometimes, too, she wished that her tame robin would hop along with her farther than to the end of the holly walk, but it never would; and one day the black cat ate it, all except a fluff of heart-rending feathers, no doubt to warn her that her desires were vain. For destiny had assigned her little intercouse with her fellow-creatures.

Once, however, she had a companion for a while. It was during her seventh summer, when her cousin Pierce Wilmot spent his holidays at Glendoula House. Just at first Eileen found this an experience as alarming as it was novel. Breakfast and luncheon became such serious ordeals when she had to confront a great-sized stranger—Pierce was about double her age and much more than twice as big—concerning whom the furtive glances she ventured upon gave her an impression of a very black head, and eyebrows as dark and straight as if they had been ruled with pen and ink. She thought he looked ferocious, and privately inquired of Norah whether holidays were *many* days.

But on the second morning, after breakfast, this forbidding person suddenly said to her: "Come along, little Bright-Eyes, and show me everything." At which address her terror culminated, and then, as terrors sometimes do, toppled over into nothing at all. A few minutes later they were going about together quite amicably out of doors. Pierce was so immeasurably Eileen's superior in age and all its privileges that he had no need to assert his dignity by keeping her at a distance—as the rabbits did—and they fraternised apace. The July morning was still freshly fair, with a twinkling trail of dew shifting along from blade to leaf up the sun-lit sward, as the moon's silver-spun wake shifts over a rippled water, and with gossamer threads, that might have been ravelled out of a rainbow, woven between furze and broom bushes, when Eileen and Pierce began to ascend Slieve Ardgreine. For one of the first things she had to show him was her stone chest. She took an especial pleasure in doing so, because she very seldom had an opportunity of even talking about it to anybody, the matter being, she felt, a family affair, which she could not with propriety enter upon except to old confidential Timothy, whose distaste for the subject she was bound to respect.

"Why, *you'll* never get up there," Pierce said with some incredulity, when, in answer to his inquiry whither he was being taken, Eileen pointed to the ridge above their heads,

"*Were* you ever up so high?" he asked, doubtfully.

Eileen would have been very sorry to let him perceive how absurd she thought this curious misconception, and she only replied: "Every fine day, if they don't say the grass is too boggy altogether. And old Murtagh says I skyte up as fast as his Cruiskeen going after a rabbit."

On the way up, Eileen gave her companion, whose life seemed to have been spent chiefly in towns, a good deal of information about common natural objects. Some of this she had excogitated for herself during her solitary rambles, and it appeared to surprise and amuse him rather unaccountably. Her explanation, for instance, of how the hedge-hogs came and stuck themselves over with the withered spines of the furze-bushes, that had dropped off mottled and grey. Among other things she showed him two or three rabbit-holes; but here it was Pierce who had new facts to impart. "So that's where they sleep, is it?" he said, "I always thought they hung themselves up like bats, head downwards against a wall; at any rate, that's how they manage in Dublin."

"That *is* funny," said Eileen; "I don't think they ever do here. And I suppose they drop down when they awake?"

"Oh, I rather fancy they never do awake," said Pierce.

"Never at all? Are you quite sure, now, that they're not *dormouses*, Pierce?" said Eileen wisely.

"Am I sure that you're not an elephant, Miss Eileen?" he said, mimicking her. "But I can tell you that if I can borrow a gun, I'll soon teach your rabbits the same trick. Why, haven't you ever been in a poulterer's shop"—Eileen never had—"and seen them hanging up?"

"Oh," said Eileen. She disliked guns and shooting, and moreover became suddenly aware that she must have displayed a ridiculous stupidity about Pierce's joke. This made her turn disconcertedly pink, so that Pierce was afraid he must have hurt her feelings, which he had not meant to do. Therefore he was glad to find, when a few minutes afterwards they reached the big stone, that she had evidently quite forgotten any little vexation in the excitement of relating its wonderful romance. He was careful to listen with such

interest, and seemingly so fully share all her
sentiments, that she very soon ventured upon
confiding to him a particular anxiety which
had of late grown up in her mind. " Do
you see what a small keyhole it has?" she
said, pointing to a little round orifice which
occurred high up on one side of the block,
and the discovery of which had been to her
a source both of hopes and fears. " Only
a tiny little *pinny* key would fit into it.
Wouldn't you think it would take a bigger
one to open a box like this?" As the hole
barely admitted the tip of her forefinger, it
could not be considered roomy, but Pierce
replied with decision: " The largest box in
the world might be opened with the smallest
key that ever was made"; and one of her
haunting fears being thus dispelled, she produced another, which took this form: " Well,
but supposing the people somehow *lost* the
key, then I suppose the box couldn't ever be
opened again, even if the person that the
things in it were belonging to did live to be
as much as twenty—old enough to be let
have them, you know?" And again Pierce
could re-assure her. " Why, there 'd be nothing
easier than to get another key made. One

takes an impression of the lock with cobbler's wax ; *I* could do it myself. So if they lose it on you, little Bright-Eyes, just send word to me, and I 'll come and settle it for you." Eileen looked grateful and relieved. " It won't be for a long while, but I 'll not forget," she said.

As they returned down the hill she said : " I wonder whether there is that very fine sort of sword in this chest too. I hope so, and perhaps there may be, only old Timothy never told me. I must ask him about it, and if there is one, Pierce, I 'll give it to you."

"And then I 'd maybe kill you with it," Pierce said, absently joking, for just at that time he was speculating upon his chances of getting a shot at the rabbits. But Eileen replied quite solemnly : " I don't believe you 'd ever like to do that on purpose—at any rate, not unless I growed up very detestfully nasty ; and you 're too big to do anything by accident." And she proceeded home, much cheered by the event of their walk.

*   *   *   *   *   *

Less satisfactory was the result of an inter-view which she had shortly afterwards with old Timothy. For, in the first place, she regretted to hear that "he couldn't be sure, but he thought it noways likely there would be a sword, or any such description of an ould skiverin' conthrivance, put up along with the good plate; at all events, he never remimbered any talk of e'er a one—not to his knowledge." And still more mortifying than this, she quickly perceived that the old butler had no liking for her cousin. What Timothy said on the subject was exactly as follows :—"Goin' out wid Master Pierce, missy jewel? Och well, to be sure, he's a fine young gentleman, considherin'. If the night's black enough, the baste's white enough, as Andy Goligher said, and he misdhrivin' home the wrong Kerry bullock." An aphorism the application of which may seem rather obscure to the undiscerning, but which Eileen quite clearly understood as an intimation that of Master Pierce Timothy thought poorly, and she was sorry for this, as she would have liked her old and her new acquaintance to be friends.

The grounds of Timothy's prejudice, however, she did not guess. The fact was that he had a few days before scowlingly from his pantry window espied Master Pierce "dis-

c

coorsin' as plisant as anythin'" with young Larry M'Farlane, "that was sister's son to ould Pather Doran, and bad luck to *him*." Now, maybe as many as a dozen years ago, Timothy and Pather had differed in a discussion about the proper season for sowing asparagus, and one of Pather's arguments had been: "That it was no great thanks to Timothy if he *had* sted a goodish while wid the Family, and he, you might say, tied to thim be the leg like a strayin' jackass." Pather's allusion was to the effects of an accident, which, met with by Timothy on the cellar-stairs at Drumlough Castle in his youth, had left him a hobbler for life; and since the controversy Pather and he "weren't spakin'." Therefore, now, if Master Pierce chose "to be great wid a one of that pack, and to go sthreelin' up the hill wid him after the rabbits," it was only natural that old Timothy should entertain no high opinion of so indiscriminating a person.

But his veiled disparagement did not check the progress of a real friendship between the cousins, and when the end of Pierce's holidays came, Eileen thought they had not been nearly many enough. On the regretful evening before he went, they paid a farewell visit to the big boulder, and, standing by it, Eileen said for-lornly: "Next time I'll only be myself."

"Perhaps I may be here again next summer," Pierce said encouragingly. He had already learned by experience that even twelve months are not interminable.

"I wish it would be next year always," said Eileen. "For that's the time when people come back. The Widow Shanahan's son's coming home from the States next year, please goodness; but she says she'll not be in this world then, so he might as well stop where he's gettin' the fine wages. Norah says that she means that she'll be dead. I wonder who told her, or how she knows. *You* don't know how soon you are going to die, Pierce, do you?"

"Not I, nor anybody else," said Pierce.

"I wanted to give her her little silver jug," said Eileen; "she's to have the little fat one that's gilt inside and has two spouts, because it's the nicest, and she's to be pitied, the dear knows, Norah says, with one thing and the other. But if she goes and dies first, I never can. Do you think she'd wait a while, if I told her about it as a secret?"

"She mightn't be able," said Pierce.

"Ah, and then it would only tantinglise her,"

said Eileen, "so I'd better not.   But I'm sorry."

"Don't forget that you must send me word, if they lose the key, and you want another," Pierce said to change the subject.

"I'll remember," said Eileen.   "But I'll have to keep on living for ever so much longer before they'll let me want it.   You see, I'll not be twenty-one even next year, I should think."

"I should think not indeed, Miss Eileen," said Pierce; "you're no age worth speaking of at all."

They were now descending the hill, and for some way Eileen mused vainly about possible remedies for this deplorable state of affairs. "I wish," she said at length, "that a great many days would happen all together sometimes —in bunches like the black and white currants, instead of one by one and one by one: ever so long they last, when there's nobody here but me.   One might get old pretty quick then. Wouldn't you like it better, Pierce?"

"Well, no," said Pierce.   "If the days were used up that way, there'd be so little time for doing anything.   Mostly they're short enough ; and there's no hurry about getting old, as you call it—an old woman of twenty—you're a queer young person, Eileen."

"I was only thinking," said Eileen, "that perhaps I mightn't be able to wait a great while, any more than the Widow Shanahan. And it would be a pity if I wasn't in this world when the chest is opened"; and although Pierce replied: "Oh, nonsense; where else should you be?" she continued to contemplate this contingency in sad silence as they trotted down after their perch-long shadows over the sunny turf with its jewelled embroideries of golden trefoil and pearly eyebright, and dim amethystine thyme. But when they had just come to the gap in the dyke, where you step across two flat stones into the highest field, a somewhat consolatory thought struck her. It was: "Perhaps, then, they'd give all those things to you, Pierce, and I've told you what everybody's to have, so mind you don't forget."

She was so engrossed by the idea that she nearly tripped over the unheeded stones, and her heir and executor, preventing her tumble, said: "Oh, it will be all right, never fear; but meanwhile, little Bright-Eyes, you'd better not break your neck. We'll both of us have grand times when I come with the key."

*   *   *   *   *   *

Eileen had many of her long years, almost nine, in fact, during which she might have forgotten Pierce and his promises, but she never did. Only once in all that time did anything happen to remind her of them, and that was on the Christmas after his visit, when Tom Roe, the postman, brought the first letter that had ever been addressed to Miss Eileen Fitzmaurice. Being opened hastily, it was found to contain a little white cardboard box, within which lay among rosy cloudlets of marvellous pink cotton-wool a tiny silver key, sent to Eileen by her cousin Pierce—her affectionate cousin, Pierce's mother, who put up the packet for him, had written him down without consulting him, as a matter of form. The gift filled Eileen with gratitude and delight. Yet, in the course of the morning, her Aunt Geraldine came upon her when she sat in the book-room window, eyeing her new possession with a somewhat doubtful countenance. "I'm almost afraid," she said half-aloud, "that it isn't quite long enough. And I never did see a key with a pin in it before."

"Long enough for what?" said her Aunt Geraldine. "It seems to me to be a very pretty little brooch, and it was exceedingly good-natured of your cousin to think of sending you one."

"Oh yes, indeed, and it is very pretty, as pretty as can be," Eileen protested. She flushed distressfully at the implication of ingratitude partly, and partly at this new view of the trinket, which would involve the vanishing of its peculiar charm. "I was only thinking," she said, "that I have poked my finger farther down the hole than this would reach; but, of course, if it's a brooch"—Aunt Geraldine had not stayed to hear her explanation; and Eileen presently put away the little box in her drawer, feeling that something had blunted the fine edge of her pleasure.

Those nine long years passed by uneventfully. It seemed, indeed, as if fewer things and fewer happened at Glendoula. In the Big House life went on somewhat in the manner of a machine gradually slowing down. Lady Fitzmaurice grew from season to season a little more invalided and melancholy, her sister-in-law more abstracted and apathetic, old Timothy stiffer and lamer in his gait. Even the ancient grey parrot on his pole in the parlour sank deeplier into his dotage, and only grimaced silently at Eileen when she tried

to start a conversation with him. Eileen herself was an exception, though perhaps poten-
tially rather than actually, the fresh spirit of
youth making less resistance than is commonly
imagined for it against the coercion of dreary
external circumstances. Still her disposition
was naturally blithe and hopeful, and she
would have been ready enough with her: O
brave new world! if any fair wind had borne
the good ship into her ken. But instead of
that she was destined to see a woeful wreck
come drifting by.

*   *   *   *   *   *

It was gradually, by an aggregation of
rumours, faint and vague at first, that warnings of the black time impending stole into
Glendoula valley, much as the wan mists creep
thither from seaward, a mere smoke-wreath
falling away down the purple-rifted shoulders
of Slieverossan, with the murk of a sky-enfolding
cloud gathered up opaquely behind them.
Felix O'Riordan, returning from Clonmorragh
fair one July day, first brought authentic news
of how "the quare ugly blackness on the
pitaties, the same that done destruction last
year on the crops away down in different parts
of the counthry, was desthroyin' all before it

now no farther off than Kilfintragh, just at the
back of the hills." And through the rainy
harvest weather ensuing, reports of the like
became as frequent as the unkindly and chilly
showers that drip-dripped unseasonably over
the little fields. Then fell a heavy thunderous
night, with flickerings of sheet-lightning fitfully
casting an evil eye through the dark, and on
the morrow, when its pall lifted, there was
grief and fear among the neighbours at Glendoula, for the sober green ridges looked as if
a scorching breath had passed over them, and
from their drooping haulms and leaves came
wafted the ill-auguring odour.

After that the trouble throve and waxed
like the most unmolested weed. A man perhaps seldom tastes despair much cruder and
sheerer than when at the impatiently desired
potato-digging he turns up spadeful after spadeful, spadeful after spadeful, nothing but dangling
lumps of malodorous slime, nothing but that
whatever, on to the very end of the drill, where
the wife stands watching him and saying : "Ah,
the Lord be good to us—have we ne'er a sound
one in it at all?" with the childer beside her
looking on, piteously concerned or piteously
indifferent. Before Slieverossan had drawn

down his winter snow-hood, the dearth wrought by the ruined harvest was finding its victims far and wide. Serious distress existed in the big houses, where people were at their wit's end to devise some agreeable substitute for that empty dish on the dinner table. Savoury rice, they tried, and stewed toast, and Yorkshire pudding, and many other such things, but none of them satisfactorily filled the place of the missing potato. There still remained a gap all-thing unbecoming at their feast. It was a dreadful loss. But in the small houses people were spared all worry of that sort at least, because when they had no pitaties, they had nothing else to eat, bad or good, which made their bill of fare a perfectly simple matter, thus illustrating, no doubt, the providential law of compensation.

Eileen's mind, however, was not philosophic enough to show her this aspect of the case, and what she did actually see and hear smote her with sorrow and dismay. It seemed as if the way of her world, hitherto a tranquil, sometimes rather tedious, one, had changed into the path of a surging flood, whence cries of despair and beseeching hands appealed to her vainly where she stood, secure herself and helpless and remorseful. So little for anybody could she do, who would fain have rescued them all. Even if she had commanded the whole resources of the household, they would have been miserably inadequate ; but as it was, Aunt Geraldine said drearily that she supposed it was no use giving to vagrants, and old Timothy, whose inborn tendency towards "naygurliness," had developed into a vice-like clamp, which acted automatically at the pressure of a petition, kept one watchful eye perpetually upon the hall-door, and another on the little store-room across the passage. Only by rare conjunctions of good luck with agility could Eileen elude his vigilance so far as to fetch and carry between them unbeknownst. More often than not, she arrived too late to do anything ; and at best, her stealthiest operations among the bread - crocks and biscuits were pretty sure to bring the old man shuffling thither in defence of the menaced commissariat.

" Arrah now, Miss Eily, what work have you there, cuttin' up the fresh loaf? and the laws bless us all, but that's the hunch! If there was a slab of a brick wantin' for repeerin' the house-wall, you could make a shift wid that."

" There's a very decent poor man at the door,"

Eileen might say, "who looks as if he had been starving for a month of Sundays; and he has a scrap of a baby with him; its mother died yesterday at Kilfintragh. I must get it a piece of soft bread, and a drink of milk, if there's any left."

"And what for need you be destroyin' a whole loaf for a crathur o' that size? Sure, I seen it comin' past me window, sittin' cocked up like a kitten bewitched. I've some stale bits in the other crock 'ud do it grand."

"Oh, those are nothing but little crumbs, only fit for the chickens."

"Musha, long life to it! And is it settin' itself up to want betther feedin' than the chuckens? Well, now, I should suppose that what's good enough for them's plenty good enough for it, when the most differ between them is that sorra the use *it's* ever apt to be, starved or no, except makin' throuble for itself and other people."

"Well, if some babies had been fed like chickens, perhaps they wouldn't have grown up so fond of gabbling like old geese," Eileen might rejoin, inaudibly, so that the repartee should relieve her own at no cost to Timothy's feelings, as she escaped with her booty.

But her raids were not by any means invariably so successful. Sometimes she found that Timothy had forestalled her, and had swept everything into an inaccessible locker; and sometimes there was really nothing left to sweep. So then she had no resource save to ensconce herself in the remotest backward-looking room, that she might not hear the interchange of entreaty and denial, nor witness the lingering withdrawal of the rejected suppliants, wandering away disappointed out of sight, but not out of mind so soon, behind the glossy-walled belt of laurels.

For a like reason she shunned in those days what used to be a favourite walk beyond the front gates along the quiet lane, with its broad green banks softly on one side mounting up into amply spreading grass-slopes, now haunted at its every turn by sorrowful spectres that she had no charm to lay. Occasionally one of them would say to her: " Ah, melady, the blessin's of God on the sweet face of you, and may you never know what it is to want the bit," and this made her feel herself all the more to be a sort of ravening locust. Her own meals, indeed, those times, were partaken of grudgingly and of necessity, after which, carrying everything she could lay hands on, she hurried off to the end of the elm grove, where a herd of small children would be looking out for them with large eyes. But day by day she thought her supplies seemed to dwindle, and the pinched faces to multiply, and she was as powerless against that as if it were the on-coming of night. One day in a week of black frost she desperately sold her godmother's cameo bracelet to a passing higgler for a shilling, wherewith she bought out of a baker's cart three portly loaves; and the satisfaction which these caused to prevail for a while, a short while, almost compelled her to think that she would dispose in the same method of her silver key-brooch, her only other ornament, the next time he came by. But always, having looked at it for some minutes, she replaced it in its box without achieving any resolve. The pencilled line, still legible on the lid, seemed to protest against the transaction in the name of the dead summer that lived with her brightest memories.

*   *   *   *   *   *

All this while the big boulder stone was lying out under the stars and mists and shadow-shifting winds on the grassy ridge of

Slieve Ardgreine; and thither constantly travelled Eileen's thoughts, although her bodily pilgrimages to it had grown less frequent than heretofore, since dripping tussocks and long, bedraggled skirts had become a graver consideration. She had never lost her faith in it and its contents. Nothing whatever had occurred to alter her opinion about it, and the silence on the subject which various reasons obliged her to maintain helped to ward off chances of disillusioning enlightenment. Eileen's sixteen years in lonely Glendoula had taught her so very little either at first or second hand about other Quality's domestic arrangements, that for anything she could tell, it might not be unusual to keep the family plate locked up in a large stone chest out-of-doors. Therefore no antecedent improbability cropped up to struggle with the existence of a long-cherished, deep-rooted dream and desire.

The one change that had here been wrought by those slow-footed, empty-handed years was in the use she designed for her riches. This change grew more radical under stress of the famishing winter. She no longer could care to admire the beauty of the bright gleaming silver things, nor to sort out from among them fastidiously appropriate gifts for each — that indeed had become only too simple a process, since everybody's need was the same. Her sole wish now was to sell all that she had straightway—she would have waited to make no pious bargains about treasure in heaven— that she might satisfy the poor with bread. But the more intensely her wishes concentrated themselves upon that object, the more keenly she felt how far it was out of reach. Four years and some months, jealously reckoned, still were lacking to her of the age that would legally entitle her to enter upon the possession of her property; and although she now knew from other sources than old Timothy that some inheritance did then await her, what could such a distant prospect avail in the face of to-day's direful necessity? Chafing sorely against the law's delay that set bars between the owner and her rights, Eileen wondered sometimes whether the Lord Chancellor, whom she understood to rule her destinies, might not under the circumstances be persuaded to trust her with her fortune, now that she was sixteen and a half, just to keep poor Denis Madden's half-dozen orphans, and old Widow Flynn and her blind daughter, and all the rest of the people from starving completely. Once she actually ventured upon a remote hint at some such possibility to her Aunt Geraldine, but lacking courage did not approach the subject closely enough to make herself intelligible; a failure for which her conscience often pricked her in the following days.

*   *   *   *   *   *

More than ever on the morning when this incident befel: It was mocking March weather, bright and calm and pitilessly cold, and Eileen thought she would warm herself by running up to her big stone, which she had not visited since the autumn. But before she reached the first bend in the avenue young Larry M'Farlane hastily met her, and turned her aside into a shrubbery with a moving story about a crippled blackbird which was fluttering there among the bushes. "Unless some ould miscreant of a cat might be slinkin' away under the low branches this minyit, Miss Eileen, wid the crathur grabbed in her mouth." Larry had invented this little fiction on the spur of the moment, the fact being that just round the turn, a few yards from where he stopped Eileen, a heap of rags seemed to have fallen, as if

D

flung or blown down across the road. Its halt there had indeed been so unpremeditated that only a remnant of the crust someone had begged hard for up at the House a minute before was still gripped in a gaunt hand. Coming upon this obstruction, young Larry, whose fare nowadays did not conduce to athletic feats, found its removal quite beyond his powers, and therefore ran on to seek help, when his meeting with Miss Eileen converted his most urgent duty into the task of hindering her from "gettin' a quare fright along of the misfort'nit poor body." He accomplished it only in part. For he could not contrive but that she should notice the gathering of a crowd in the avenue, and the shrilling of shocked ejaculations, and then the bearing away with slow solemnity, which apprised her of how near the cloaked shadow had passed.

Eileen gave up her expedition to the stone chest; its baffling impenetrability seemed just then a cruel gibe of Fate, wiselier ignored. Larry, for his part, temporarily lost sight of the errand which had been bringing him up to the Big House: a commission he had undertaken to execute for the postman. Thus

it was not until the evening, when the cold
March twilight had faded, too tardily for
many people impatient to huddle away into
oblivious sleep, that a letter reached the
thriftily-lit drawing-room, where Eileen and
her aunt were also getting through the interval
before bed-time as best they could, which
was but dully. A letter was something of
an event in itself, and this one, unlike most
of its predecessors, did not collapse inanely into
a listless "Oh, it's only"—for it contained a
real piece of news.

Glendoula was to have another visit from
Pierce Wilmot. Pierce, who had grown up
a civil engineer, was now in charge of certain
road-making relief-works, which were about
to come creeping down Letterglas valley
and up through the Nick of Time into the
neighbouring glen. The superintendence of
these would bring him to stay for a while
near the place, and he hoped to renew his
acquaintance with his kinsfolk at the Big
House. All the establishment was more or
less thrilled by the intelligence. It seemed,
of course, only natural that he should take
up his quarters there, and the prospect pleased
on the whole. Lady Fitzmaurice, even, and

her sister-in-law were slightly cheered and roused; even old Timothy, despite his prejudice, set about his polishing with a revived zest, in anticipation of a visitor who might be expected to appreciate "the differ between spoons that had a proper shine kep' on them, and ones that was as dingy as if you'd loaned them for stirrin' the Ould Fellow's tay." All the others, who remembered Master Pierce as a fine friendly-spoken young gentleman, thought that it would be a pleasant variety to set eyes on him again, and the rest were quite ready to welcome him on that recommendation. Eileen alone looked forward to his return somewhat doubtfully. She knew right well that things could not be the same as they were in those very olden days; and the differences might not be improvements. Suppose that she did not like the grown-up Pierce, nor he her? Then her reminiscences, she thought, would be superseded and spoiled. Still, she believed herself, after all, to be glad that he was coming.

*   *   *   *   *   *

It was late on a wild bleak evening that Pierce arrived, after a long open-air day of surveying and supervising. An additional pair of candles illuminated the drawing-room in his honour, and were burning clearly enough to show what manner of man he was at four - and - twenty. He had not changed at all irrecognisably, being still black and straight-browed, alert and rather resolute-looking, as beseemed a person whose business consisted largely in the clearing away of obstacles, by summarily forcible methods if need were. He had done this figuratively upon occasion as well as literally since his last visit to Glendoula. But the little girl who then used to patter up and down that primitive path beside him was now much harder to identify, having shot up so slender and tall. Also in Pierce's honour, Eileen had put on her best gown that evening, a fine white muslin, sprinkled with a pattern of little lilac rose-bunches, outlined in a cloud of black dots. It was not more than half a decade lag of the latest Dublin fashions, but the six months' growth since its last wearing had certainly made its skirt a rather skimpy length, as she noted with chagrin when putting it on. Some consolation was found in fastening her deep embroidered collar with the silver key. She had plaited her brown hair, darker now, yet keeping its richness of latent gold, in an unusually elaborate Grecian-plait to coil in a careful spiral knot at the back of her head. But first it framed her face in satin-sleek bands, smoothed down low on the delicate curve of the cheek, and then gathered up, leaving on either side a loop discovering a shell-like ear. As pink as a geranium-blossom one of them was that evening, the nipping cold and her thin dress had tempted her to sit so near the fire; and her eyes were as softly bright as ever, with such light as a sunbeam, questing beneath leaf-lattices, may waken in a moss-brimmed nook of clearest well-water.

Pierce noticed all these things, and none of them, while he was greeting his Aunt Geraldine; and he fell in love so simultaneously that it would have been impossible to say whether his observations came before or after. His habit was to be prompt and decided, and with promptitude and decision did he grasp this new experience—of which, nevertheless, an access of very unwonted diffidence and irresolution seemed part and parcel. These set in immediately, as if he had passed a vote of want of confidence against himself upon the spot, and its effect was retrospective, throwing a slur alike upon his present and his past. He wondered whether his cousin had not thought him a peculiarly odious schoolboy. His old pet name for her suddenly occurred to him as persistently appropriate, but the mere remembrance of it made him feel so over - presumptuous that he almost wished her to have forgotten it. In like manner he recollected, and could not dare to remind her of, their climb up Slieve Ardgreine, or their adventure with the strayed goats, and other episodes. He had retained only just enough common-sense to understand that Eileen's silence all the evening upon this, and indeed every other topic, was not intended for a rebuff; and the flow of his conversation with his Aunt Geraldine was not a little impeded by a perpetual apprehension, altogether superfluous, of her niece as a critic.

Of course, he was not very long in recovering his presence of mind. In a day or two he began to dispense with such hampering precautions, but the sentiment that had suggested them continued in full force, and did not cease to influence his behaviour. Less, perhaps, in his dealings with Eileen than with the world at large, it made him transpose himself, so to speak, into a softer key. He unlearned in a single week some tricks of peremptoriness and self-assertion, which the vicissitudes of one early set in authority had been teaching him through several past years. For it was with him as if he had suddenly discovered the existence of something precious and perishable, that a touch might shatter or a breath destroy, and thereupon he grew wonderfully sensitive to the wide - spreading intricacies of cause and effect. How could he tell but that a rough word spoken any-where might set a-stirring peril-fraught vibra-tions to reach and threaten the head that he loved? For her sake, he would have liked everything to be on velvet, and he was always instinctively aiming at that end. The most unskilled and incapable of the labourers whose efforts he superintended found their miscel-laneous inefficiency treated with singular forbearance, even if it attained an egregious-ness characterised by their comrades as "a quare botch intirely," and driving their foreman to demand of various powers, celestial and otherwise: What to glory the great gaby was at? During leisure moments their lank and hollow-eyed gang were prone to pass the remark that "the captain" was "a rael gintleman"; while up at the Big House all the inmates accorded him all sorts of golden opinions.

Eileen herself meanwhile was not in the least aware of what had befallen him, but she had left off dreading any detriment to her cherished memories, and his visit had undoubtedly brought an influx of pleasure and interest to cheer her present day. She was so unaccustomed to being made much of by relations that this kinsman's good nature impressed her as quite extraordinary, and so little used to making much of herself that she never thought of attributing it to anything except a special quality in Pierce, rather more likely, no doubt, to be exercised in another person's behalf than in her own. It repeatedly surprised her to see that he remembered and acted upon her opinions and wishes, as if they were really important — a new view of them which she would have been slow to adopt. One morning he rode off all the long way to Denismore and back to get her Alfred Tennyson's latest volume, and her delight in it was alloyed only by the intrusive consideration of how much coarse meal the price of it would have purchased. For her mind was still engrossingly pre-occupied with the neighbours' trouble.

*   *   *   *   *   *

The cloud of it had lifted a little since Pierce's coming. Possible wages loosened the famine-grip on such households as could send forth a man to ply pick and shovel, instead of hopelessly lying abed "agin the hunger"; and then a spell of more genial weather inter-posing released everybody from the clutches of that other icy-fingered foe, whose co-operation is so deadly. "For sure," as old Christy Shanahan had been known to remark in this connection, "to be starvin' inside and outside at the one time is more than any raisonable man can stand at all, unless be good luck he was a graven image." This dim lightening of the prospect, however, rousing a stir of hope where numb despair had begun to prevail, made the need of plans for a timely rescue seem all the more urgent. One evening at dinner, Eileen heard Pierce say that if the people could get food enough to ward off the fever just until the potatoes—

supposing there should be any—were dug, they might do well enough ; otherwise, it was a bad lookout. And he added that it was hard to see how it could be managed, as the road-making grant had nearly run short, and where else should the money come from ? At that Eileen had almost spoken her haunting thought aloud, and it was: "the great chest full of silver." And though the unpropitious moment enjoined silence, therefrom dated the designing of an enterprise so venturesome that the possibility of carrying it out was a point upon which she hopefully and fearfully changed her mind a dozen times daily for as many days.

At last there came a brilliant, capriciously-lighted morning, with its shine and shadow under the control of a shifting snow-drift, which sailed at the wind's will. It was a holiday, and Pierce succeeded in setting out almost as soon as he wished on the early walk he had planned with his cousin. What slight delay did intervene was caused by the arrival, just as they were starting, of the Widow Barry with a couple of eggs to sell on commission for her next door neighbour—the Widow Shanahan, who "could get that far be no manner of manes herself, the crathur."

"And they're the last ones you'll be takin' off her, Miss Eileen, she bid me tell you," said Widow Barry. "For she's after killin' her ould hin this mornin', because it's torminted she was to be seein' it mopin' around starvin' the same as a raisonable body, sorra a bit had she to be throwin' it this great while back whativer. 'Deed now, you might as well be walkin' along the shore of the say these times as along be the dures down the street, for e'er a scrap of pitaty-parin' or anythin' else you'd find lyin' about. The crathur had to be contintin' itself wid whativer it could pick out of the ground, and bedad I won'er it had the heart to think of layin' e'er an odd egg at all. So she took and wrung its neck this mornin', and she said the sup of broth 'ud keep the life in herself and poor Katty for a day or so anyway. But och, Miss Eileen dear, it'll be the weeny sup entirely. For 'twas meself caught the crathur for her, and I declare to goodness it wasn't the weight in me hand of a little wisp of hay. Sez I to her, the feathers on it 'ud be heavier be thimselves. But sure she could do no betther; and if it boiled into the name of broth even, it'd give them the notion they was aitin' somethin'." In prospect of this repast, the sixpence that Pierce sent seemed to him hardly more than an emphasising of a "strong distemper and a weak relief"; but the Widow Barry, who went her way filled with a gratitude to God and man, may have understood the situation better.

And then the two young people set out on their rambles. They took their old favourite route up Slieve Ardgreine, for the first time since Pierce's visit, on Eileen's part, as the milder weather had been "soft" too, turning the mossy nap of the turf into a treacherous sponge, that squelched coldly over-shoes at the lightest footfall. To-day, however, it might be traversed dry-shod, given a discreet avoidance of extra vivid patches in the golden green; and a busy thirsty breeze had left scarcely a dewdrop in the glazed cups of the celandines and the pink-rimmed saucers of half-blown daisy-buds. Up this daintily carpeted path Eileen picked her steps rather silently. Her companion thought that she had been saddened by the incident of the ill-faring fowl, but that was not the reason. What pre-occupied her was the great venture which she appeared to be approaching more or less in spite of herself. The very direction which their walk was taking, at no choice of her own, was like a hand beckoning imperiously. On the way up she hovered towards the verge of it, and recoiled from it, and came stealing back to it again, oftener than the flitting clouds furled and unfurled their shadow-mats at her feet; and the big boulder, the stone plate-chest, hove in sight while she was still wavering. Failure would be so very terrible to her. She knew that if Pierce were shocked or indignant, or even amused, she would be miserable indeed; and she could not by any means convince herself that he would not be all these things. Yet, when they were standing beside the tall, blackish shape together, just as in old times— only it used to be the taller then—she felt desperately that, chance what might, she must not go away without speaking the sentence she had been mentally rehearsing all the week. It rang in her ears like a clamorous bell, and made her deaf to any other speech, so evidently that Pierce stopped in the middle of what he was beginning to remark, as if she had inter- rupted him. Just at that moment the sun swam out clear of a high-tossed drift, and sent a golden wave sweeping widely up and down the hill-slopes. It broke against the big stone,

shining into Eileen's face with all the dazzle-
ment of an April forenoon, and she accepted
the omen as if it had been the cordial clasp of
some encouraging hand.   Before the radiant
rim had slidden on many paces farther, she
took heart of grace, and the irrevocable word
was spoken.

   *   *   *   *   *   *

"There was one thing I wanted to ask you
about, Pierce," she said.   She had moved
round to the opposite side of the chest, and
was looking at him across the lid, with eyes
very bright and wistful beneath her broad-
brimmed straw hat, which had brown ribbons
tied in a bow under her chin.   "I shouldn't
wonder if you thought it very dreadful of me,"
she continued ; "but I really don't think it is
myself.   After all, I only want to use my own
things, and that can be no great harm ; and if
these don't belong to me now, they don't belong
to anybody, which is absurd.   At any rate, it
couldn't possibly make any difference worth
speaking of to those people up at the office
in Dublin, and it would make all the difference
in the world to the poor people here ; so 'the
right of it over-leps the wrong of it,' as old
Murtagh Reilly used to say."   She was

gradually arguing herself into courage; still a mere shadow falling anywhere would have routed it.

"I hope it is something truly appalling, or else I'll be horribly disappointed now," Pierce replied, a little puzzled by this prologue, but rather pleasantly so, because he liked her to consult him. "You've raised my expectations cruelly. . . . But if you wish, I'll undertake not to think it very dreadful, nor dreadful in the least degree," he added, as after a short pause she seemed still to be hesitating. He would have said that he had never made a safer promise.

"Well, then," said Eileen; "do you remember how you said one time that you could easily get a key for this old chest of ours? Here's the key-hole, you see, all right. I've always kept it clear of moss. And, I wonder, would you mind—if it didn't give you a great deal of trouble—getting one for me now? Without telling anybody else, I mean, for of course they wouldn't let me. I know I can have no legal right to take anything out of it until I come of age; but that's only the *law*, and really when people are starving, one can't be expected to wait for years and years just on account of such nonsense. At the best of times it seems a great pity to keep it lying here useless for so long, but now it's like locking up other people's lives. If I can't get at it in time to do anything for them, I might as well never have it at all—there'll not be a soul left in Glendoula. You've no idea how hateful it makes one feel. Sometimes it seems to me that I'm nearly as bad as the wretches who go on carting off their wheat and oats to sell in England. Only it isn't my fault in reality, for until you came I never had a chance of speaking to any possible person about it. And then, Pierce, I was thinking that when we have got this opened, you'd maybe help me to manage about selling the silver. It must be worth a great deal of money: enough, at anyrate, to last while they are waiting for the potatoes; for we really had very fine plate, I believe, though it mayn't be quite so splendid as old Timothy used to declare—he *is* a little given to romancing. And, of course, these times I don't expect to find the yards of pearl and ruby ropes that were in the *Glittering Hoard!* You do re-member that I told you, and that you promised about the key, don't you, Pierce?" she said

E

anxiously, perplexed by his expression, for he was looking hard at her with a sort of bewildered blank dismay, almost as if something had frightened him—an effect which she had not included among her many apprehensions.

He was taken wholly unprepared, because during her irresolution Eileen naturally had shunned the perilous subject, and he had himself for the time being entirely forgotten the existence of that old childish myth. But now he did indeed remember it, as clearly as if it had happened yesterday, instead of all those long years ago. There had stood the little girl eagerly telling him her absurd story, to which he listened with amused forbearance, thinking to himself that he must not vex her by incredulity, and carelessly noticing how swiftly her small face flushed, and how brightly her large eyes shone in the excitement of her narrative. And to-day the same thing seemed coming to pass again—but with differences. For here unchanged in the sunshine was the dark stone block with its yellow dappling of lichen, and that same clear voice came to him across it, speaking so much in earnest that the transparent flower-flush rose and the glance brightened just as of old. But the small child had grown into a tall maiden, and her voice was the one that gave meaning to all the other sounds in his world, and her absurd story no longer amused him in the least, seemed liker breaking his heart, seemed the pronouncing of an evil spell, that blurred the light of his eyes, and conjured up a web of black forebodings over the fair horizon of his future.   If the soft-aired spring morning had suddenly began to scowl and keen around him, and sting him with frozen pellets, it would have faintly shadowed forth the transition.   A man's mood, however, may fall from one level to another in much less time than it takes to tell, and Eileen thought his answer came quickly.

"Don't you know that you're talking nonsense, Eileen?" he said.

She had never heard him speak so sharply, almost roughly—not even when he had seen his case of mathematical instruments dropped by Hughey Brian into the bottomless bog-hole, nor when he had come upon the Donnellys' little goat tethered with the remnant of an urgently-needed and long-sought measuring-line.   And she was imme-diately aware that the very worst had befallen.

Her plan was impracticable, and she had disgusted Pierce by proposing it. The poor Glendoula people must starve, and her cousin, who had been so good-natured, could never like her any more. Probably he considered her request worthy of a dishonestly-minded idiot, and was deeply, perhaps justly, offended at her suggestion that he should take part in such a transaction. Certainly, he would not hear of the scheme, so all her hopes were scattered like mist before a hurrying wind, and there again loomed the grim trouble ahead, with its inexorable face turned unveiled upon her. Just at that moment, however, it was partially screened by the interposition of a still uglier one, which would thrust itself between, asking and answering a question with the same tormenting result : What must Pierce be thinking of her ? He had surely meant worse than " nonsense."

Amid this rude crowding in on her of disappointment jostling with grief and morti- fication, Eileen clung half-consciously to the sense that it behoved her by all means to retain the footing of her self-possession, and she replied very gently: " Not exactly nonsense, I think ; but perhaps—I daresay it

would be quite out of the question to take
these things now, and not even right. It
seemed to me the only way I could do anything to help the people, but of course I
knew it mightn't be possible at all. I don't
understand much about the law. Don't you
think it's getting rather cold up here?
Perhaps we'd be wiser to come back before
the day clouds over."

This dignified composure seemed to Pierce
as it were a seal set upon his fear, the
document of which her fantastic story had
supplied, and he dejectedly turned down the
hill-path with her in silence. The sullen-
looking stone which they left behind them, a
blot on the sunny sward, might have been a
little ancient altar to some unpropitious God,
whence they were taking home, sorrowfully,
discomfortable oracles. In truth, one of them
had there said farewell to an old hope, and
the other struck up an acquaintance with
a new fear; both experiences apt to arouse
pre-occupying meditations. Neither of the
cousins gave much heed to their surroundings
as they went. The small wild clouds flirted
the sunshine about as if flocks of white wings
were flickering by; here and there they flung

down the shadows which make one marvel
how their "little-seeming substance" can be
the cause of such deep purple stains. But
now nobody marked them, nor the far-off
pipe of the plover, nor the fragrance of the
basking herbage underfoot.

Thus they presently came to the gapped
dyke leading into the first field, and all the
way neither of them had spoken a word.
Now, at that moment it happened that Eileen
was looking very straight before her, with her
head held rather high, and her eyes steadily
opened, to give the tears a chance of going
back the way they had come, and walking
warily as one who felt how even the quiver
of an eyelash might be fatal. Yet these
precautions defeated themselves, for they were
the reason why she stumbled at the flat
stepping-stones, so that Pierce had to save
her from falling just as he had done nearly
nine years before. This time, however, he
did not let her go again with a laugh. He
held her close and said: "Oh, my darling, my
sweetheart, don't be vexed, don't be vexed.
It will be all right, never fear. We'll pull
them through—all of them—safely somehow.
Don't think about that old silver any more;

and you won't mind what I said just now?
I'm a stupid brute, you see, sweetheart; but
there's nothing on earth that I wouldn't do
for you."

While she listened to this statement, Eileen
went through, in an intensified form, an
experience somewhat resembling that of the
bygone summer morning when the unknown
Pierce had first spoken to her: a sudden
surging up of dread, that wave-like took her
off her feet for the instant, but only to lift
her unharmed into a new world, most beauti-
fully strange, and shut out from all troubles
of the mere earth with the light that never
was on land or sea. A reflection of it in
her eyes encouraged him to pursue that line
of argument, and he said a great deal more,
all much to the same purport, as they went
down the steep green fields, where the young
bracken - fronds were uncoiling their flossy
silken whorls beneath last season's weather-
beaten brown plumes, and the golden blossom-
flakes were melting off the tall winter furzes;
and then on between the fledged boles of the
elm-grove, and under the scented shadow of
the laurel-walk, until at the hall-door Eileen
ran away to make a solitary survey of the

unexplored regions in which she had wonderfully arrived. Just for the moment Pierce felt gratefully disposed towards the big stone, which had, at all events, given him his cue.

＊　　＊　　＊　　＊　　＊　　＊

But later on that afternoon he spoke very bitterly to his Aunt Geraldine, whom he found alone in the book-room. The hearing of candid opinions is a privilege not uncommonly enjoyed by spinster aunts.

"You've kept her moping here all these years," he said, "without companions or amusement or occupation, till it's no wonder that she has taken up queer fancies. Why, it was enough to drive her—to make anybody unlike other people. Surely you might have managed better for her somehow."

"It really wouldn't have been easy," his aunt said, but meekly on the defensive; "we always have had so little ready money, and then your poor Aunt Gerald's wretched health is another difficulty. Besides that, I never noticed anything odd about Eileen. She always seems contented and cheerful enough, and I thought she was a sensible sort of child, and very quiet. Just once or twice, now that

I think of it, she has said something that rather puzzled me about a plate-chest, but I had no idea she had any delusion of the kind."

"Yes, that's just where it is; nobody has cared to look after her or take any trouble about her," Pierce said, wrathful and reproachful, a little unreasonably; so fresh was his discovery that concern for Eileen's welfare ought to be the prime consideration in every rightly ordered mind. He did not surmise, either, that he was upbraiding a friend. Yet such was the case. For, from the very first evening, their Aunt Geraldine had guessed whither things were tending, and ever since had been watching their course, a melancholy sort of Prospero, who was powerless to work any wonders, and whose joy at nothing could be much, but who did feel some pleasure in the growing likelihood that her favourite sister's son would some day reign in the wreck of the old place, and take charge of the person whom she had always regarded half-pityingly, half-impatiently as "Eileen, poor child." Therefore the cropping up of this ominous obstacle was a disappointment by which she felt so cast down that she had not the spirit to rebut with any energy the accusation of contributory negligence.

Neither she nor Pierce had spoken of the circumstances that lent the matter its menacing aspect, but they were uppermost in the mind of each. What made Eileen's futile story sound so warningly in their ears was the remembered existence of that baneful spectre whose mischief might be traced among the annals of the Fitzmaurice family, as well in the notorious eccentricities which had preluded poor Sir Gerald's last desperate act, as in the more or less pronounced oddities and deficiencies which had wrought the history of this kinsman and the other into a tragedy with a grotesquer plot.

" I can't think what has put such a notion into her head," Miss Fitzmaurice said dejectedly. The workings of Eileen's mind could hardly indeed have been more remote from her observation if they had gone on in a different planet. " But, after all, Pierce, if one considers how young she is — scarcely more than a child."

" No reasonable child would believe anything so preposterous," Pierce replied with gloom. " A rough lump of a boulder with moss growing in the cracks ! "

" And did you tell her so ? " asked his aunt.

"Well, no, not exactly; we began talking about something else, and I thought I'd better see whether you knew anything about it; but apparently you don't," said Pierce.

"Oh, you must just laugh her out of it," his aunt said, laughing nervously herself, and had not any more helpful suggestion to offer. Pierce left the interview dissatisfied and unreassured.

*   *   *   *   *   *

Towards sunsetting, however, he found himself once more on the summit of Slieve Ardgreine. He had promised to go and see after Barney Foyle, who had been "took bad wid the road-sickness" on the day before, and as the Foyles' cabin stood by the side of the Clonmoragh road, his shortest route was up and down through the Nick of Time. The sight of the solitary boulder, squatting there starkly black amid the flushed western glow, made him realise his trouble with much searching of heart. It seemed a symbol, or something more than a symbol, a visible tangible embodiment of the obstruction which had thrust itself into the clear path of his desires. Now, Pierce Wilmot was alike by nature and training a person who could not, without great and grudging reluctance, admit impediments to his progress along the way wherein he would go; and in this case he felt more loth than ever before. As he crossed the stretch of sward towards the gap, he eyed the dark mass with a hot thrill of resentment, as if against somebody who had wittingly baulked and baffled him. Yet withal it was for him so obviously nothing more than just an ordinary lump of limestone, that in view of it Eileen's quaint belief took a stronger tinge of unreason. Nor did he possess, to soften it down, any knowledge of how the seed had been sown in her mind, and had grown up, fostered and never disturbed, through the long years of a lonely childhood. So, for a few paces, his heart sank and sank, till it reached depths where a poignant pity was the most endurable element in his mood.

But before he reached the Nick of Time, an idea that flashed across him made him deviate several yards to the right, and walk up to the big stone. He stood still beside it, reflecting for a while, and then gave it a slight kick, as though to mark his arrival at some definite conclusion. At that moment he was saying to himself: "In any case it would be better out of this; and I'll do it the first thing to-morrow, by Jove I will! Then I'll bring her up here, and the chances are that when once she's seen it in fragments she'll never give the matter another thought. There was that young fellow the Barnards knew, who got rid of a curious hallucination in much the same sort of way. They burned an old paper on which he had taken it into his head that the safety of the whole world depended; and when he found that nothing happened, he grew perfectly rational about it. And so will she. For indeed she's as sensible as anybody can be, except just on that one point, which won't signify an atom, if it's taken in time. It's a good job the notion occurred to me. Ay, that's the kind of key I must get you, sweetheart—poor little Bright-Eyes. However, I'll take good care that she shan't be vexed about it. So there'll be a short end of you, you old *stookawn*, and joy go with you," he said half-aloud, with a defiant flourish of his black-thorn towards the big stone, which, as he turned his back upon it, flung a long, murky shadow after him, like a scowl, over the sheeny grass.

*   *   *   *   *   *

The next morning did not smile upon anyone's undertakings; rather, it might be said
to survey them unsympathetically through a
blank, expressionless mask. For Letterglas
and all its neighbouring glens were full of a
white fog. It was not merely the soft mist
that clings about distant tree-clumps and
cabin-clusters when the sun is still low, and
uncurls slowly, peeling off from round them,
while he climbs, giving one an impression that
the landscape is a fragile work of art, not yet
quite finished careful unpacking out of delicate
cotton-wool wrappings. All the night through
a vast white cloud had been adrift thither from
the westward, over seas, hanging low always,
and sometimes trailing on the very face of the
water like a huge disabled pinion. Beneath it
the dim blue tide had crept to the limitary
foot of the cliffs, furtively, as if from an
ambush; but the wavering ribbon of weed
and froth set no boundary for the thronging
vapour-masses, which passed on wafted inland
through rifts and over crests, till at length
the escorting breeze dropped and left them
halted motionless, a crowd checked by invisible barriers. Round about Glendoula they
made all the valleys into one, spanning the

ravines with ghostly causeways and bridges, and levelling the peaks, lost among aërial snowfields. The curd-white impenetrable wall looked at a few yards' distance so dense and solid that the thought of walking through it almost took away one's breath, and people about to emerge from it loomed along with such dim, unsubstantial shapes that their voices sounded startlingly loud and near.

Yet, notwithstanding these obstructive conditions, work was going on in Letterglas valley, where wheel-barrows trundled to and fro invisibly, tilting out clattering loads, and picks swung unseen till one stood close to the wielder's elbow. Pierce, the inspector, had made his way thither, gropingly, at an early hour, having a special job in view, which he was anxious to get done as soon as might be. But since a field of vision wider than the present was desirable for his operations, he consulted the weather-wise among his men as to the probability of the fog clearing off. In old Murtagh Reilly's opinion, which was highly esteemed upon such points, this might be expected to take place before they were much older.

"I wouldn't wonder if it was very apt to

be givin' itself a heft agin we're done breakfast, your honour," he said ; "and once it fairly gits a rise on it, it won't be long streelin' itself off out of your way. It's quare somewhiles to see the rate them mists 'ill be skytin' up the hillside at, and not a breath of win' stirrin' that 'ud thrimble the feather of steam whiffin' out of an ould kettle's spout, let alone liftin' a big cloud fit to thatch a townland."

"Sure it's the sun shinin' on the wrong side of them does be drawin' them up," said Christy Martin instructively, "like as if they was a wet shirt shrinkin' in front of the fire. The flannen's a terror for cocklin' up into nothin' if the hate's too strong for it."

"I dunno where the great likeness is then," said old Reilly, who had not a taste for instruction.

"Maybe there's not, Christy," said Christy's brother Willy ; "very belike there is not. But all the same, you and me'd be glad enough of a pinny for ivery time we've seen the sun comin' out red on this side, lookin' the livin' moral of a hot cinder burnin' through a blanket."

"Have it your own way, lads," said old Reilly, sublimely abandoning the whole expanse of the heavens to them with a comprehensive flourish of his hand. "Howsomiver, your honour, if you was axin' me, I'd say this day's apter than not to be takin' up prisintly, or next door to it, as thick as it is this instiant minyit."

Old Reilly seemed to have said truly, for by the time that everybody rose from the sodded bank, on which some of them had been eating slices of bread as they sat—others were in the same plight as John O'Mahony, who remarked humorously that it saved a dale of throuble to have your breakfast yisterday or else to-morra—there was a perceptible curtailment in the flowing drapery of the hillslopes, and a thinning of its texture, paler shimmering brightness running through it here and there, to show that the opaque folds might shake out into diaphanous tissues of pearl and silver.

Accordingly, a small knot of men by-and-by detached themselves from the rest, and began to ascend towards the Nick of Time, whose gap was still hidden by an ample curtain. Pierce was one of the party, which carried up with it a supply of gritty black grains and sundry coercive-looking tools. He invited Murtagh Reilly to accompany them, but the

F

old man cried off the expedition. "I'm thinkin' I'll stop where I am," he said, "for these times when there does be a notorious curse on the counthry, and the hungry-grass growin' over ivery inch of it, troth it's as much as a man's life's worth—and if that's no great things, it's the most he has—to be settin' his misfortnit fut e'er a step further than he's bound. But you've a plinty of the lads along widout me, your honour."

* * * * * *

Just at the same time, Larry M'Farlane also set off up the slope, by a different route from the others, however, and with a different goal. He was taking the shortest way to the Big House down at the bottom of Glendoula. The fog there had begun to recede a little earlier than in Letterglas, but still muffled things very closely, making mysteries of the most familiar objects, and Larry, who, to judge by his headlong bounds and plunges all the way, might have been racing for at least his life, collided more than once with a tree-trunk when he came among the plantations. And he reached the house panting, only to run up against more hampering blocks of delay. For in the kitchen was nobody except Mrs Dunlop,

the cook, busied with frizzling preparations for
the breakfast, and all she could be got to say
was, "Aw, ax Mr Gabbett, Larry man ; he'll be
apt to know if she's after goin' out, and if she
isn't, she might be indures yit." And when
he rushed on to the pantry, old Timothy, who
had overheard the voice of an unfavoured
visitor, shot the bolt of the door, and was long
deaf to all thumps and calls. In fact, Larry,
the urgency of whose errand divided every
minute infinitely, was turning away in despair,
when the old man shouted a surly, "What's
a-wantin?" and he had to waste another tormenting interval before a churlish chink opened.

"Wantin' to spake to Miss Eileen?" said
old Timothy. "Then want'll be your master,
me hayro of war, for I seen her goin' out
a while back. So if that's what all you had
the prancin' in the passage for, like a cross-
tempered carriage-horse kep' standin' in a
could win'——"

"Murther alive and wirrasthrew and bad
luck to it," Larry said, "what'll I do at all
now? And which way did she go, Mr
Gabbett? Was it up Slieve Ardgreine she
wint, do you suppose? For it's biddin' her
keep off goin' up it I'd be."

"Well to be sure, and set you up Your-self's the great one to be givin' your orders. And how the mischief could I be tellin' you where she's went, except be the sound of the hall - door clappin'? But I dunno what'd take her sthreelin' very far up the hill, unless she was wishful to lose herself body and bones in the thick of the fog that you might take and cut like the side of a rick. And if you're from the place where they're workin', sure you'd ha' met her comin' along, supposin' she's gone that way."

"I might ha' passed her by twenty times over unbeknownst, up about the top of the fields, where you couldn't see a goat's horns and tail together," said Larry; "nor I wasn't keepin' along be the path the most part of the way; I just slapped down the shortest I could. But if I'd had the wit of an ould blind crow, I would ha' sted on her own path, and then I might ha' stopped her. But I'll be hard set now to git a chance of findin' her at all."

With that, Larry bolted away too hurriedly for any further questions, thus frustrating the curiosity of old Timothy, left wondering "What for in the nation the bosthoon would be warnin' Miss Eileen off the hill," a riddle for

which he could invent himself no plausible
answer.

*   *   *   *   *   *

Larry's surmise was partly right, Eileen having
in reality been on her leisurely way up Slieve
Ardgreine while he sped hot-foot down it.
She had slept little in the night, and would
have almost grudged that little, had it not been
for the pleasantness of waking to the recollection that she was not only dreaming. The last
time she did so, the silvery lines framing the
shuttered window, though but faint as yet,
convinced her that it could not be too early to
get up. Rising, she was fascinated by the
spectacle of one of the snow-whitest and
stillest fogs she had ever seen in the dozen
years or so during which she had been capable
of meteorological observations ; and she stood
looking on at it for some time. But when the
fabric of the spacious pavilion began to give
ground a little and sway to and fro, restoring
glimpses of a substantial world and shifting
them away again, no longer contented with her
watch from the window, she determined to run
out and survey more thoroughly this rare aspect
of things. On the way downstairs she stopped

to tap at her mother's door, very softly—a velvet-suited bee would have made more noise flying against it — hoping to be let in, and fearing to rouse a sleeper. An answer did set out to her, but the feeble drowsy voice failed to reach her, so she stole on cautiously, a little sorry that she must put off her good morning until she should return. Eileen was wearing a favourite blue and white mousseline-de-laine, and had not forgotten to fasten its collar with her silver key. Over her head she had thrown a grey woollen shawl, because the April morning air was soft rather than warm. It was a somewhat shabby old shawl, and Eileen vainly reflected that if she met anybody she could just slip it off and be carrying it on her arm.

Anybody might be coming down the hill home to his breakfast about this time, and the long aisle of the elm-walk, where the straight trunk columns showed themselves momentarily and vanished as the mist-wreaths floated and melted through them, was weirdly alluring. When Eileen had followed it to its end, she found another vista opening before her out on the green slope, closed ever and anon, and temptingly cleared again by capricious wafts of dimness. For as she went there was setting in a general movement among all that great gathering of vapours; their assembly was lingeringly breaking up; a spectral city going to wrack. Vast cloaked and hooded shapes seemed curtseying ceremoniously to one another from opposite sides of the glens, while here and there some loftily towering pile might be seen to betray the frailness of its structure by a shivering from top to base like that of a sail in a veering wind. But hardly a breath was stirring in Glendoula, so that the dispersion proceeded by very slow degrees, with many fitful pauses.

Eileen's little footpath led her so closely in the wake of a receding cloud-wave that she could watch the bracken-plumes emerge frond by frond from its filmy borders, and descry the gold of the furze-blossom glimmering through the white, before the sombre branches became visible. On either hand, low trailing fleeces were caught and carded into filaments on tussocks and bents and briers. Farther up it seemed as if a spectral net cast over the hills were being hauled in with torn meshes teased and tangled. And behind all this shadowy shifting drifting there were vague motions of light, hinted at by sudden wan shimmerings of the canopy that screened it.

Eileen was always half intending to turn back, yet she went on and on, sometimes noticing these things, and occasionally stopping to gather a shrivelled dandelion bud, or a russet plantain head for the old moping parrot in the parlour at home, until at last she knew that she must have come near the stone chest. It had no bitter associations for her now. Rather she would have looked upon it as the auspicious starting-point whence she had fared to the highest fortune. Even the failure of her scheme for producing a relief fund did not any longer grieve her, for Pierce had undertaken that help would be forthcoming, and to Pierce's keeping she had transferred herself, responsibilities and all, which she found a wonderful ease to her mind. So light of heart, indeed, it made her that she now began softly to sing a sorrowful little ditty, which she used long ago to hear crooned by her poor old nurse, who had a turn for sentiment :

*" Oh sunny blooms Slieve Cryan, where the gold boughs
        creep together,*
With honey on the high cliff in ten thousand bells of heather.
*For the morn that fears no morrow is there bliss in flower
        and bee,*
*And in one heart sorrow, sorrow, for the hope that wafts
        to sea."*

But as she sang, in a voice small and sweet, of this heart sorrow, she looked on before her with shining eyes, very sure of seeing all she wanted to crown the moment's gladness come presently to meet her from among the shrouding white mists.

   *   *   *   *   *   *

Hidden among them just then, not many yards away, half-a-dozen people were at work around the big boulder, digging and boring, with frequent mention in their discourse of needles and trains and matches. Their operations were by this time, however, nearly finished, and after the last of them, which was the kindling of a lacklustre red flare with a sheet of grease-stained brown paper, the whole party withdrew hastily through the Nick of Time, and retreating some little distance down the slope on the other side, stood still in apparent expectation of an event. It happened very soon. First a fierce sharp-edged clatter, that crashed into a booming roar, followed by a duller sound of rushing thuds, as if a scattered flock of unwieldy birds had swooped down close at hand in headlong flight. An abrupt silence succeeded, for few echoes gossip among the Letterglas hills. It must have lasted unbroken for a long minute at least. For the men had re-entered through the gap, where they found the fog thickened by a sulphurous reek, and Pierce, making out amid it the expected new vacant place, was considering how he would now hurry home and fetch Eileen hither as soon as possible, that there might be no further delay in the clearance of their pleasant path—"my sweetheart," he was saying to himself with a remorseful remembrance of her sad eyes yesterday—when the air filled, the wide world filled as if it could never empty again, with a shriek and a shriek reiterated, shrill and wild, you could not have told whether man's or woman's, hardly whether a human being's, it was a skirl of such sheer despair. Yet Pierce thought he recognised in it a name that snatched away his breath.

"What was that, man? What is it?" he said, pulling the sleeve of Paddy Murray, who was nearest to him.

"Somebody's hurted for sartin," declared Paddy.

But this was probably a mistake. The fragment of the big stone that had struck Eileen on the temple, seemingly had thereby opened for her and shut the dark door, whose threshold the senses may not cross, all in an instant, before the happiness could fade out of her face, or the little bunch of carefully-gathered weeds drop from her hand. It might, by the way, be feared that poor Polly would enjoy no more such feasts henceforward to the end of his tedious days.

Larry M'Farlane it was, arrived with his belated warning, who had raised the outcry on beholding this proof that his panic-stricken hurry had been all bootless, and that the evil dream which had possessed him ever since he casually overheard talk of Mr Pierce's project was come most terribly true. Some of the others now bade him whisht and run for Dr Blake and Father O'Connor, who might both of them very belike be below at Denroche's cottages, where the Maddens and young Joe Hanlon were mortal bad last night; though, for the matther of that, it was aisy enough to see there'd be little anybody could do here — goodness pity them all. But as there was nothing else whatever that Pierce could do — he who used to be so ready with resources—he fixed his mind upon their coming with a desperate grip, while he stood by and waited idly.

* * * * * *

He felt bewildered, chiefly by the sameness of most things, which were unaccountably going on much as they had been doing a minute before, when Eileen could have spoken to him. The white mists were still curtseying to one another across wider spaces in the valley, and the dim light behind them grew slowly stronger. There was a scent of turf-smoke on the air from a fire which someone had lit under a bank a little way down the hill. The very strokes of old Dan Heron's hammer continued to come up in a faint rap-tap from the roadside, where he was break-ing lumps of reddish sandstone; for Dan was so deaf that he applied himself to his tasks with abstracted concentration, and could not easily be interrupted. Evidently the news had not penetrated to him. A murmur of voices was passing to and fro in a knot of men gathered at a short distance. Pierce might have caught a sentence now and then.

"You'd a right to ha' sent them word to keep out of it—you had so—the way she'd niver ha' come widin raich of harm."

"Sure, we was intendin' to get it done that arly there'd ha' been no fear of e'er a sowl about; 'twas the fau't of the divil of an ould fog delayin' us."

"Ah, now, but it's the woful thing, however it come to happen. And she the on'y one her poor mother has. Is anybody runnin' down to tell them?"

"Och you may depind—half-a-dozen."

"Well, it's a quare ugly world she's took out of any way, the crathur, God knows. 'Deed now, I do be wonderin' somewhiles what He's at wid bringin' the likes of her into such a place at all."

"And small blame to you to be wonderin' that same,' Jim, if it's for nothin' betther than to take and knock the bit of life out of her, as if it was a gossoon slingin' stones at a little wran hoppin' along in the hedges."

"That's no sort of talk. God be good to the crathur, she looks as if no great harm was after happenin' her any way."

"It's not kilt at all she is, I'm thinkin'. The Docther's apt to say she'll be finely agin prisently."

"Bedad now, you might ha' more wit, man— Och, it's on'y poor Crazy Christy."

The sound, but not the sense, of this discussion reached Pierce, and vaguely irritated him, because he thought it might prevent him from hearing the approach of what he forced himself to imagine possible assistance. But when Father O'Connor, not long afterwards, did come up to him, it was with no more practical suggestion than: "God help you."

"*God?*" said Pierce. "What on earth can God do? I think it has killed her." He put his question like one assuming some self-evident proposition, and the kindly old man turned away from him with a shake of the head, and no attempt to gainsay.

The next voice to arouse Pierce's attention was that of a youngish woman, worn and weather-beaten, whose grey ragged shawl hooded black wings of hair, and the dark eyes that often look out so full of cares from such surroundings. He recognised her as Norah O'Neil, by birth Kinsella, and she was saying: "So I thought maybe the Docther might be up here, Mr Pierce—but sure it's all one. There's nobody can do a hand's turn for him or any of us now, on'y God. For himself's lyin' dead too, sir, be the roadside down beyant the bridge. And, truth to tell you, it's quare set agin stirrin' out he was this mornin', wishful he was to be lyin' in his bed, for he said he felt cruel wakely in himself altogether. But it's losin' the day's wages I was thinkin' of, and settlin' to call him all the lazy hounds I could lay me tongue to —poor Mick, that was good to us ever—for 'fraid we'd be starvin' to-morra. So he went off wid himself. And the God that's above me knows well, on'y for the childer I wouldn't ha' said a word. But, Mr Pierce, the faces of thim is gone to nothin'; there isn't a one of thim the width of the palm of your hand. And on'y for the childer, to be lavin' thim, God knows I'd liefer be lyin' the way Miss Eileen is this minyit, instead of her, the Saints in Heaven be good to her, that's the young crathur. Many's the time I've carried her up half-ways to this very place, when I wasn't so much oulder meself. For what else will I be doin' all the rest of me life, but remimberin' the day I dhruv poor Mick out of the warm house to get his death on the roadside, when all the while I knew in me heart he wasn't rightly able to stand on his feet. And he——"

But Norah's story was here jostled aside by Con Furlong, the foreman, a stolid, business-like person, who wished to mention that the men were all quitting their work, and to receive instructions about paying for a couple of loads of stones that were just after coming over from Smith's place beyond Clonmoragh, where *he* had never ordered them. These details some-how helped Pierce to realise more fully that he was to be still alive. Meanwhile the sun had found a clear path earthward among the mists, and shone out through them with all the glamour of dawn and splendour of high-noon, so that swift lights strode hither and thither upon the hills, and the haze melted into the deepening blue as fast as foam on a summer sea, until the spring-day was golden over the whole countryside. It was just the world and the weather for those grand times which, as Pierce now suddenly remembered, he had promised that Eileen should have when he came with the key.

A DESERTED CHILD

A DESERTED CHILD

THE Round Lodge at Kilrath is so ornate
a little structure, with its pillared portico
and fantastic pagoda-like roof, that it looks
as incongruous in the lonesome grass-lands,
amongst which it is solitarily set, as a single
pelargonium or calceolaria would look among
their ragweed and thistles. Only the old
people recollect how it was built by way of
being a gate-lodge on one of the new roads
which there was talk of young Mr Hall
making at the time he came into the property, but which, like many more of his
schemes, were never carried out. None of
them, in fact, ever took a substantial form
except the Round Lodge, his promptness in
this matter being caused by a long-standing
promise to his old nurse that if he succeeded
to the Kilrath estate she should have "a little
house of her own." As his regard for the old
woman was one of the few interests he had left
unshrivelled by the gambling fever that had
fastened on him, he found an eager pleasure
in keeping his word to her, and travelled all

the way down from Dublin that he might be present at her induction into her new abode.

It was a moteless morning in early summer, when the curved masses of the wood still had a misty softness of hue, and the green of the fresh lawns looked as unwitherable as the domed blue above them. The Round Lodge gleamed most spick and span within and without, its brilliant tiles glowing, and the violet and amber panes in its glass door richly staining the sunbeams that crowded into the little porch. Mrs Moran, glancing round the cosy sitting-room with bright quick eyes like a bird's, felt herself happy indeed, though she only *said* she dared say she might make a shift to manage well enough, once she had the things set to rights a bit herself in her own way; which would have sounded faint praise to anybody who did not know her. But when she was left there to her own devices, she became subject to fits of forlorn "lonesomeness," at intervals which grew shorter day by day as the first gloss of ownership wore off. It did so the more rapidly because the Round Lodge was so far out of the way that she seldom had a visitor to whom she could exhibit her possessions with proud dis-

paragement.   We all like to look at our own
happiness through other men's eyes, a process
by which it seems to gain a sort of stereo-
scopic solidity.   Her nearest acquaintances
were the old coachman and cook couple who
lived as caretakers in the gaunt, empty
mansion two miles away ; for though the
village is considerably closer by, a bit down
the road after you turn out of the boreen,
anybody who supposes that Mrs Moran could
have associated on terms of intimacy with
its inhabitants must be sadly to seek in
a knowledge of our finely shaded social dis-
tinctions.   Mrs Dowling alone, who was
mistress of the post - office and shop, and
who wore a bonnet at Mass, might have been
an appropriate crony, but she was at this
time "mortal bad wid the janders."   Hence
the clear summer noons and nights often
strung themselves into a whole week without
giving Mrs Moran an opportunity of saying
anything more to the purpose than the
occasional "Fine day, ma'am," which even
neighbours who are not acquaintances must
exchange when they meet.   This was a dull
state of things, and made the hours wagged
out by the bland-faced clock lag and loiter

strangely. Sometimes, if she had not recollected that she was at last in the long-desired
little house of her own, she would have
almost thought she had been in better
places ; and satisfaction that has to be conjured
up by an effort of memory comes cold and flat.

A few perches to the westward of the
Round Lodge a belt of timber breaks the
smooth sweep of the broad pastures that
encircle it. If you thread the narrow footpath between the delicate grey beech-trunks
for quite a long distance, you come to the
edge of a high bank, which overhangs a deep-
sunken lane, a mere boreen joining two more
important thoroughfares. Thence the trees turn
at right angles to fringe the brink of this lane.
Across it you look into a wild country. The
great Shangowragh bog rolls from the horizon
almost to your feet, and on the right hand,
towards Lisconnel, spreads far away, a spacious
level that seems brown until you have called
it so, and then you see many other colours
struggling duskily through, olive and purple
and red. To the left there is rougher ground,
mottled with grey-gleaming boulders and
clumps of furze, and lifting itself up lazily
to a stony ridge. Beyond that rise darkly a

pair of domed mountain summits, the same
that are seen more dimly from Lisconnel.
Here they have the aspect of two huge hooded
heads, bowed over a mysteriously folded
hollow. When Mrs Moran came within view
of this landscape, she generally shrank back
among the sheltering trunks, and went home
the way she had come. She said it made
the flesh creep upon her bones, and she
wouldn't stop where she'd have one of those
ugly black-lookin' blocks of hills grimacin' at
her from mornin' till night, not if she was
paid for it by the hour. The fact was that
she had lived all her life in the corner of a
softly contoured up-and-down county, where
the little rounded grass hillocks and frequent
hedges make the countryside look as if it had
been crumpled into green bunches, and where
the prospect seldom extends over more than
a few hawthorn-bounded fields at a time. So
that these vast stretches of wilderness were
for her a new and startling revelation of
possibilities in Nature, which she was somewhat
disposed to resent. On the whole, though she
would by no means have allowed it, even to
herself, the little house of her own was more or
less a disappointment, and disappointments that

occur when one is verging on threescore-and-ten have a discouraging air of finality.

But with that first long summer at the Round Lodge, Mrs Moran's solitude was ended by the arrival there of her daughter-in-law, Mrs Peter, and of her three grandchildren, Nannie and Biddy and Con. Their coming was caused by a very tragical occurrence, and apart from the melancholy circumstances, I doubt that it added to the old woman's contentment. She had long since made up her mind that she would not like a bone in her son's wife's skin, and the prejudice did not melt away upon acquaintance, while the children were rather oppressive to her after her long holiday from such society. Since the infancy of Mr George, now in the Lancers, she had scarcely seen a child to speak to, in the grown-up Halls' deserted nursery; and she said aggrievedly that they *moidhered* her, and that ne'er a one of them featured their poor father. Nannie and Biddy, good-natured, hot-tempered little girls, shocked her by their romps and quarrels; and four-year-old Con, a small, melancholy child with a turn for metaphysics, caused her some chagrin by his unthriving aspect; she said that he looked like a hap'orth of soap

after a week's washin', wid the face on him
no broader than a farthin' herrin'. With all
their shortcomings, however, the young Morans
were presently the means of bringing a still
less promising inmate to the Round Lodge.

About this time Kilrath happened to be suffer-
ing from a visitation of the Tinkers, who had
established themselves as usual in the row of
deserted cottages at the end of the boreen. The
Tinkers were people who spent all the tolerably
warm part of the year among the benettled wall-
rims of deserted cabins, and under the arches
of bridges, and in the hollows of old quarries,
making progresses to and from these quarters
with the help of two donkey-carts. Most of the
party passed the heart of the winter in the less
primitive shelter of whatever Union workhouse
was nearest when the first unbearably cold night
overtook them. Now and then a member of
their confraternity disappeared for a space into
the more rigorous seclusion of some county jail,
but that was an accident of occurrence less common than their temporary neighbours could
have wished. For the Tinkers, it is said, stole
all before them. Middle-aged inhabitants of
Kilrath remembered when the band had filled
only one cart; but of late years they had over-

flowed into a second, the owners of which were known as the Young Tinkers. It was considered that the Young Tinkers were collectively greater thieves of the world than the Ould, but that no single individual could hold a candle for villainy to Luke Maguire, the very ancient commander of the original vehicle. People wondered sometimes that the Young and Ould Tinkers did not part company, and take different routes, as their joint arrival at any camping-ground was generally the signal for a frantic fight between the two sections. However, they continued to stick together, which, as a Kilrath housewife remarked, was " a rael charity, for if they took to scatterin' themselves over the whole countryside, like a flock of turkeys in a stubble-field, she should suppose there wouldn't be a hin or an egg to be had in it from one year's end to the other."

So not long after the Peter Morans' establishment at the Round Lodge, the Tinkers sent to the door a deputation composed of a woman and two children, all wildly ragged, and hung about with samples of their flashing tinware in such profuse festoons that their approach sounded, one may suppose, somewhat like the onset of a mail-clad knight of

old romance. Their call was but brief, for
their appearance did not favourably impress
the two Mrs Morans, who were afterwards
careful to exhort Nannie and Biddy and Con
that they must on no account have anything
to say to "them young rapscallions," if met
with on their walks abroad. The little
Morans, who had been staring with all their
eyes full of envious admiration at their two
contemporaries permitted freely to handle and
clink those resplendent and resonant cans, felt
vaguely the existence of compensations and
complications in the scheme of things, when
they learned that these privileged persons
were nevertheless to be shunned as somehow
inferior and reprehensible, and "not anyways
fit company for respectable people's childer."

But on the next Saturday their mother went
to shop in the village, and up at the Round
Lodge the children found the morning as long
as mornings can be when one is under seven,
and the end of an hour is out of sight. By
the time that Nannie and Biddy and Con had
finished their midday dinner, they felt quite
convinced that if their mother meant ever to
come back to them at all, she must now be
somewhere near at hand ; and while their grand-

mother was busy washing up, they slipped
away to meet her along the path among the
beeches. It was a pleasant autumn day, with
crisp leaf-drifts to scuffle underfoot, and here
and there a more or less ripe blackberry attain-
able, amusements which drew them on until
they reached the brink of the abrupt descent
into the boreen. They saw no sign of their
mother coming, and the bank looked so very
high and steep that they could not even think
of climbing it. But while they strayed desultorily on the top, somebody, swinging from
clumps of weeds to handles of looped roots in
monkey-like fashion, came suddenly scrambling
up it, and then squatted down cross-legged under
a sloe-bush. The new-comer seemed to the
children a very large person, being a well-
grown girl of ten or eleven. Her dress consisted of a brown skirt, which looked as if it
had once been a sack, with a man's old jacket
for a bodice, eked out by a screed of greenish
shawl. She was barefooted and bareheaded,
with a great shock of black hair making thick
eaves over her brows, under which her light-
grey eyes shone like the gleam of pools caught
through dark-fledged boughs. This was Judy
Flower, eldest daughter of Jack Flower, head

of the family of the Young Tinkers. Strictly
speaking, Jack's surname was Murphy, but
Jack's father, who had enjoyed some local
renown as a wrestler, had been styled by his
admiring neighbours "The Flower of Clon-
moyle," and his children had been spoken of
as the Young Flowers, until the nickname
hardened into a patronymic, which Jack took
with him when he sank into the tinkering line.
Judy's mother, on the other hand, had real
gipsies among her ancestry, which was, perhaps,
the reason why Judy sat cross-legged, and had
something weirdly Oriental in her aspect.

The Moran children sidled away a few paces,
eyeing her doubtfully; but she took no notice
of them, and began to eat a bunch of remark-
ably large and ripe blackberries, evidently the
remains of much similar spoil, for her hands
and lips were blue with juice-stains. When
she had finished them all but the last, which
was also the biggest and blackest, she suddenly
held it out to Con, saying, "There's for you,
young feller, and a grand one it is—a dew-
berry. Stuff it in your mouth, and no more
talk out of you." She spoke in a high-pitched
gabble, and with a peremptoriness of manner
modelled upon that used by her elders to

herself. Con was half scared, and Biddy plucked Nannie by the sleeve, whispering dismally, " Let's go home, she's ugly-lookin'." However, the plump - seeded, glossy berry proved irresistible, and Con's hesitation ended in a furtive grab. Nannie, emboldened by this mark of confidence, came a step nearer to Judy, and said, peering down the bank wistfully, for her gleanings by the way had only served to whet her appetite, " There would be a dale of berries in it over yonder ? " Judy craned her neck round the bush, and looked down the bank too, and then at the the three small children, who stood in a row. " Is it berries you're after ? " she said, " and is it over there you'd be goin' ? Whethen now, if you knew what all was in it over there, 'tisn't about berries you'd be talkin. Och no, murdher alive, not indeed, bedad."

" Over where is it ? " said Nannie, im-pressed and alarmed by the redundancy of Judy's asseverations.

Judy pointed up the boreen, which just there turned sharply, and under a roof of reddening boughs formed a vista, ended by the dark mountain-wall. " Och if you was after seein' the laste taste of a sight of a one of them"—she said, with appalling vagueness. "Och mercy on us all and more too, if you on'y was."

"What sort seein'?" said Nannie, with increasing anxiety. The row had shortened itself considerably, the children had shrunk so close together.

"Crathurs," said Judy. "Och my goodness the crathurs. Tiger-bastes, and camel-horses, and mambolethses—rael frykful. I cudn't tell you the half-quarter of their. But the crathur of all the crathurs is the big red snake that's in it. Awful *he* is. Och the dear help us, I hope he'll bide contint where he is, I hope he will. Wirrasthrew, if he was to get hearin' any sort of noise that 'ud wake of him out of his sleep —whoo-oo, that'd be the bad job for us all."

The children stared at her round-eyed like a bunch of fascinated little birds.

"Well now, but it's the terrible big red snake *he* is," Judy went on contemplatively, "and the great hijjis lump of a black head he has on him; it wouldn't scarce fit in between them two bushes; and the long len'th he is, that'd raich aisy to the far end of the boreen—and he asleep up yonder, ready to wake every instant minute of time that happens—and bould little children talkin' of leppin' down the high banks after blackberries."

"We worn't," said Biddy, with a howl.

"Where is he asleep at all?" said Nannie in a hoarse whisper.

"Sure, up there in his black hole," said Judy, pointing through the trees, "wound himself up he has—round and round and round-an'-round-an'-round"—she described a rapid eddy in the air with her forefinger—"wid his big ugly head cocked in the middle, listenin' till he hears somethin' to wake him up—and then, good gracious, is it what'll he do?" she said, replying to an interrogative gasp from Nannie, "Murdher alive!" She ducked down until her shock-head nearly touched the ground, and recoiled immediately to an erect sitting posture with a jack-in-the-box-like spring. Then she elongated her neck preternaturally, and twisting it from side to side, glared about her with a ferocious goggle and grin. "That's what he'll do first," she said, "to find out what way the noise was comin' wakenin' of him. And after that, he lets a couple of roars out of him, and he begins to unrowl himself—round and round an' round-an'-round—the wrong way. And as soon as he's stretched his len'th, out he'll take wid himself slitherin' down the hill to us, and through the trees there he'll come smashin' desthruction off of all before him. Ragin' mad he'll be for bein' woke up. Och the creels of him and the crawls of him," said Miss Judy, rocking herself to and fro, so that the withered leaves on the thorny bush behind her fell over her like a shower of little golden coins, "och the creels of him and the crawls of him, and the roars of him and the bawls of him —there was never anything aquil to it. 'Twould terrify the clouds out of the sky. . . . And mercy be among us, what was that at all now? Was it him beginnin'? I dunno but I heard him over yonder, like as if he was sayin' *cruel* to himsel, 'Whoo-oo-o, let me be comin' at them.'"

This was too much for the fortitude of Biddy, a small fat child with no great force of character, and she broke into an uncontroll-able roar, to the wrathful despair of Nannie, who shook her passionately, saying, "Whisht, whisht, you little madwoman! do you want to have us all destroyed?" Con, on the other hand, not less dismayed, flew frantically at Judy with a snatched-up stick, confusing the causer with the object of his terror. Judy herself rose to her feet, and resorted to pre-

H

cipitate flight, not by reason of Con's assault, but because at this moment a voice called shrilly through the trees, "You young miscreant there, what at all are you doin' wid the childer?" It was old Mrs Moran, who, alarmed by the stillness, had set out in quest of her grandchildren. Judy, who had no wish to explain the situation, sought to escape from it by a hasty retreat down the boreen bank, but her attempt was unlucky. For in her hurried swinging of herself over the edge, she trusted her weight to a tuft of ragweed, whose roots ripped faithlessly out of the crumbling soil, and let her drop amongst a scattering of earth and pebbles into the middle of the lane, where she lay stunned and incapable for the present of any further romancing.

It was in this way that Judy Flower became an inmate of the Round Lodge, being carried up their by Michael Kelly, a turf-cutter, who appeared opportunely on the scene. He then tramped off several miles to summon the doctor, observing as he started that there was likely to be an Inquist to-morrow. But when the doctor came, he pronounced the case one of merely slight concussion of the brain, and predicted a rapid recovery, if the child were properly cared for, which Mrs Moran resolved that she should be. "The crathur might stop where she was for a few days at any rate, till she came round a bit."

The Tinkers themselves did not display much concern about the fate of their youthful comrade. On the evening of the accident, two of the women came to make inquiries at the Round Lodge, and their report seemingly satisfied Judy's family, for next morning the whole party decamped, moving on in the direction of Castlebawn. But it had happened that just at this time Judy's mother was absent, tramping the country on a professional tour, with a baby and a bunch of tinware, and so heard nothing of what had befallen her daughter until she rejoined the caravan at Castlebawn. They picked her up in a dreary little back lane, where she awaited their coming, seated on a broken-down mud wall. Her tin cans were nearly all slung about her still, but she had nothing in her arms, for the baby had died of bronchitis in the cold weather the week before, little to anybody else's regret, perhaps not even its own. But the event had disposed Mrs Flower to take a tragical view of things, and therefore, when her family equipage creaked near enough to admit a counting of black and red heads, which showed that one was missing, she immediately formed the gloomiest conclusions about the fate of the absentee. Nor were the explanations she received particularly re-assuring. Little Jimmy, her eldest boy, reported that Judy had fell off of the top of somethin', he didn't rightly know what, and hadn't come home since. And his aunt Mrs Massey's account of the matter ran: "Och, sure she's after givin' herself a crack on the head, but the ould woman that picked her up off the road was a dacint body, and she's took her in. She might get over it and do right enough yet. Anyway, the best chance was to lave her where she is. It's late we are, for the roads is that heavy they're nearly pullin' the hoofs off of the misfort'nit asses' ould feet. How did she get the crack? Sure the on'y wonder is she hasn't broke her neck a dozen of times wid the way she climbs over all before her. And so the baby's died on you? Ah the crathur, God be good to it! 'Deed now, it would be cruel knocked about in the perishin' weather. Belike it's better off. Did you sell anythin' at all? Musha then, woman, you needn't be

frettin' after Judy, for she's apt to play plinty
more fool's thricks yit, if that's all ails you."

Mrs Flower was, however, bent on not only
fretting, but going to see after and if possible
repossess herself of Judy. She was ill and
miserable, and had been looking forward to
the close of her weariful, lonesome tramp, and
a spell of easier days, jogging along on wheels
among familiar faces. But Judy was the
eldest of her children, and had perhaps never
quite lost the glamour of a wonderful new
possession, which her mother could not contemplate in another person's keeping without
a pang of jealousy. At any rate, she made
up her mind to resume her solitary way, and
she kept her resolve despite the disapproval
of her family, of her gaunt-looking husband,
who said she'd a dale better stop wid the
childer and him and mind them a bit, and
of the childer themselves, who, feeling mocked
and defrauded by a glimpse of comfort so
speedily withdrawn, howled dismally and
drummed protests on the sides of their cart,
as they saw the much-desired wisp of black
shawl recede fluttering down the wet street.

Under these discouraging circumstances,
aggravated by wild wind and rain, Mrs

Flower started on her doubtful quest. Four days she had to trudge in solitude, and three nights she had to shelter as best she could, the best being on two occasions no better than the lee-side of a dyke and a clump of rustling furze-bushes. Such wide tracts of bogland intervened between cabins where a night's lodging may generally be had for the asking, because the indwellers have little else to bestow. But she consoled herself with the hope that on the way back she should have her daughter's company. She durst not now face the possibility of "anythin' havin' happint Judy," so that she would after all return alone. That would have been to look recklessly down a gulf of despair. So she allowed herself to doubt of nothing except her chances of reaching her goal before she was perished outright, or "took rael bad intirely." When she came to the village of Kilrath, a wannish gleam of prosperity flickered out on her, for she succeeded in persuading Mrs Nally, the owner of a stray spare penny, to buy a tin mug, which was described as being "that iligant and polished up, 'twould be a pleasure to drink anythin' out of it, if 'twas on'y a sup of ditch-water, and strong? Och goodness preserve us,

ma'am dear, you might take and batter it agin
that wall there the len'th of the day, and sorra
a dint there'd be in it when you'd done." As
she knew that the Round Lodge could not be
very far off, she expended the proceeds of
this sale in purchasing a little flour cake for
Judy at the shop. It was richly yellowed with
soda, and showed three currants on its surface, which could not fail to tempt the most
delicate appetite. "And sure the bit of a
crathur would be finely agin now."

By the time that Mrs Flower came to the
Round Lodge, the wintry dusk had thickened
so that the driving sleet-sheets were more felt
than seen. The leafless beech-grove was roar-
ing in the wind with the voice of a foam-fretted
shore, and straining and swaying to the stress
of the blasts until it looked like an anchored
cloud. She groped baffled among the dripping
trunks for a long while before she found a clue
in a line of red light to guide her across the
dim grass-field, until she stood under the porch
of the Round Lodge. It was the Tinkers'
habit to be stealthy in their movements, and
she passed through the coloured glass door
unheard, and down the short passage to where
another door stood rather widely ajar, revealing

an interior of ruddily lit warmth, paradisiacal to anybody peering in very cold and wet and hungry. Only Mrs Moran and Judy were in the kitchen, which glowed all round its curved walls so that the room looked like a cupful of light filched from the ebbing day. Judy, now convalescent, installed in one of the fine new arm-chairs by the fire, with locks clipped and combed, and wearing a neat lilac print frock and little plaid shoulder-shawl, was wonderfully transformed in aspect. She was eating a broad slice of buttered griddle-cake, and listening to a long story, which Mrs Moran had drawn from her store of reminiscences about the Quality she had lived with. While Mrs Flower watched, the old woman got up and brought the girl something in a large mug. "It's a nice sup of buttermilk for you," she said; "sup it up, honey, along wid your cake. I declare now, you and I are great company together intirely."

"Ay are we," said Judy complacently; "and if I had me strip of knittin', I might be tryin' did I remember the stitch you was showin' me. Sure none of them at home could do knittin' no more than the crows in the field. And what become of Miss Lily's grey horse?

They'd be apt to put it out of that, after it
doin' such a thing."

Judy's mother never heard the answer to
that question, for she was pre-occupied by a
struggle towards a difficult resolve. When it
was formed at last, she turned to slip noise-
lessly away. "Sure she has her chance there,
me jewel," she said to herself. "I'll let her be."
But she was not destined to depart unin-
terrupted. As she turned to go, one of her cans
swung, clanking against the door-edge, and
Judy had espied her before she could retreat.

"Why, there's me mammy!" Judy said.
"It's comin' she'll be to take me home." Her
exclamation began jubilantly but ended in
a minor cadence, for her present quarters
were in most ways very much to her mind,
and being still less vigorous than usual, made
her feel all the more loth to resume the rough
faring upon which she looked back across this
brief novel experience of cosy chimney-corners
and ample meals. It struck her that her
mammy might have arrived more appropri-
ately some other time; *some* time, of course,
but *other* certainly; and the opinion betrayed
itself on her countenance.

"Well, and what way are you, Judy?" said Mrs

Flower, pausing as she found herself observed ; "grandly you look to be set up in there, bedad."

"Oh, she's doin' finely?" said Mrs Moran. "You'd better step inside, ma'am—if you're Judy's mother," she added, though she could not forbear a mistrustful glance from her visitor's bedraggled rags to her own clean boards and good bit of carpet. "It's wet walkin' to-night."

"I dunno but I'd a right to stop where I am," said Mrs Flower, standing still. "Drippin' I am, sure enough; the showers this day'd drinch a water-eel. I was on'y trampin' round wid the things; and as for takin' you along, Judy, 'deed for the matter of that, sorra the hurry I'm in at all, unless them that have got you so be."

"There's no hurry whatsomever," said Mrs Moran rather stiffly. "Let alone that the child's noways fit to be streelin' about the counthry."

"The saints above know I've no wish to be saddlin' meself wid her," said Mrs Flower defiantly. "It's just a livin' torment she'd be to me, and divil a hap'orth else."

"Well, to be sure, one'd ha' thought you might ha' found somethin' more agreeable to say of your own child," said Mrs Moran, "even supposin' it isn't convenient to have her along wid you these times."

"Convenient, is it?" said Mrs Flower.   "Be jabers, it's them that has the rarin' of the likes of her knows the throuble of it.   Troth, you might be tired bangin' her about and givin' her abuse from one day's end to the other, and get no good of her at the heel of the hunt."

"'Deed then, if you can conthrive nothin' better to do wid her than that, I'd a dale sooner she sted where she is," said Mrs Moran, with increasing sternness, and a change of mind about the propriety of offering Mrs Flower a cup of tea.   "She's an unnatural crathur," she said to herself, "and all she cares for is to be shut of the child."

"Well, good-bye to you, Judy," said her mother.   "I'll not come near you, I'm that muddy and wet."

"But you'll be comin' back some time soon, mammy?" said Judy, who had hitherto kept silence, somewhat shocked and affronted at her mother's disparagement, which was a new experience to her, as at home Mrs Flower had been always wont to defend Judy's character and extol her, without much cause, "for lendin' a great hand wid the childer," and other domestic virtues.   Now, however, Judy was stricken with remorse as she saw the familiar black shawl and weather-worn face disappearing into a darkness which led towards the dreary noises of the wild night. She got out of her arm-chair, and despite Mrs Moran's remonstrance, ran across the room and down the passage, hobblingly, because she was still lame from her fall. When she reached the porch, her mother, though close by, was almost swallowed up in the gloom, which had superseded the last glimmers of twilight. Only in the farthest west lingered a dull red band, hardly more luminous than a drift of the dead beech-leaves. Judy stood on the steps peering out, with the hearth-glow behind her. "Stop a minute, mammy," she called; "I 'm after forgettin' to bid you good-bye or anythin'. And I 'll ax herself inside to be wettin' the tay——"

Mrs Flower looked round, and halted for a moment. Then she shook her fist menacingly at her daughter. "Be off and run in wid you out of that, you young divil!" she shouted hoarsely. A gust of wind intercepted and bore away the words, but her threatening gesture was plain enough against the fading wraith of the sunset. And it was the last that Judy ever saw of her unnatural mother.

AN ACCOUNT SETTLED

AN ACCOUNT SETTLED

ONE wet autumn evening, Mr Natty Grogan was taking stock and making up his books with the assistance of his family. When thus occupied, the young Grogans were wont to complain that he would be trotting after them with dogs' abuse from Billy to Jock, till you couldn't tell where to have him; while he used to declare that the lot of them all together were more different kinds of fools than you'd find anywhere else in the breadth of Ireland, and so was their mother before them. She had died many years since and her husband was reported to have re-marked that the event would save him a couple of shillings a week, anyway, for milk and chicken-broth. But it is fair to observe that unfeeling speeches were likely enough to be put into his mouth on this occasion—such was his character among his neighbours. They said that his wife had been " a very dacint poor woman, and a dale too good for any such an ould slieveen, and it was a pity all the childer, except, maybe, Andy, took after himself."

For the present, however, popular disapproval of the Grogans was in abeyance, as almost everybody else had gone to bed and to sleep, so that Athcrum's one wide street lay deserted and blank. It was a very wet evening, and the whitewashed house-fronts had an ample dado of mud splashes about their doors and lower windows, but they were all now muffled up in darkness. The Grogans' late sitting threw no light on the outer gloom, for the battered shop-shutters were up, and business proceeded in the little back room, whence old Natty lit himself every now and then with a sweeling dip, to grope among his stock-in-trade in the adjoining shop. He accompanied these researches with dissatisfied grunts, rising occasionally into requests wrathfully shouted to his family, for an explanation of what he found or missed. They grimaced at one another, and sometimes whispered together before they complied with his demands—Nannie and Tom and Stevie, seated round the table, where the strong lamp-light flared in their faces. Their father, peering in at them from murky recesses behind the counter, half saw and half surmised these signals, which did not soothe his irritation.

"What at all's gone wid the rest of the
the ten-pound tin of arrowroot biscuits?" he
called suddenly. "It was better than three
parts full last time I seen it, and, accordin'·
to the accounts, there's no right to be anythin'
out of it since then, but ne'er an atom have
you left in it, on'y a dust of crumbs."

"Belike *they* niver put down the last person
had some," suggested Tom, disassociating himself from the transaction with prompt presence
of mind.

"And why the mischief didn't you? Am I
keepin' the pack of yous foolin' here to be
slingin' me goods about the parish, and not so
much as take the trouble to scrawm it down?
There's not an infant child goin' to school but
'd make a better offer at doin' business."

"It's very apt to ha' been Mrs Moriarty,"
said Nannie, choosing to ignore this aspect
of the matter; "she did be gettin' them kind
of things the time the childer was sick. We
can aisy charge them to her."

"Mrs Moriarty's great-grandmother's cat!"
said her father. "You might as well save
yourself the trouble—and there's none readier
—of chargin' anythin' to her these times. The
people at the post-office was tellin' me this

I

mornin' that the last American letter come for her, sorra the money-order was in it at all, except word of the daughter bein' in hospital, and the husband out of work. It's one while before she'll be settlin her account. Howsome'er, charge the biscuits to her, and don't be makin' too free wid allowin' her anythin' else on credit. Whose bill's that you're makin' out there, Stevie?"

"Yourself's after biddin' me get Dan Farrell's," Stevie replied.

"Ay, did I? It's the best chance we have to be gettin' anythin' out of the man, and he wid his couple of bastes in at Kenmare fair yisterday. If we don't look out sharp, his story'll be that the agent took the price off him for rint. The divil mend the both of them for a pair of thievin' villins! Sure Widdy Rourke below was tellin' me she seen Dan diff'rint times comin' out of Carmody's as hearty as anythin'; and when's he had a glass from us at all? Ah, musha! long life to him. A great notion he has to be spendin' his ready money at Carmody's, and we to be givin' him credit for everythin' else he happens to fancy. Plase the pigs, I'll learn him the differ! What's the amount he's owin'? Eighteen shillin'? Then just set him down

a couple of pound of them biscuits, or anythin' — the way there'll be no bother wid
change comin' out of his note."

"Biscuits he didn't get, I'll take me living
oath," said Stevie confidently.

"Keep your oaths till they're axed for.
'Twas as apt to be biscuits as anythin'. And
I'll tell you what it is, me young shaver, *you*'ll
step over to Farrell's to-morra mornin' and get
the bill ped." Old Natty gave these com-
mands in a triumphant tone, meaning them to
be a penalty for his son's contumacious con-
tradiction; and Stevie did say grumblingly—

"Troth and bedad, it's nicely bogged a
man'll be thrampin' them roads after these
polthogues."

But the young Grogans had a way of pos-
ing in aggrieved attitudes from motives of
policy, and the commission was really much
to Stevie's mind, the office of collector being
always in request among them, because it was
endowed with what they called their chances.
These consisted in a private lengthening of
the bill by addition of sundry fictitious items,
the price of which the inventor pocketed.
Thus, on the present occasion, before Stevie
went to bed he was careful to supplement Dan

Farrell's account with the following entries, which were purely efforts of imagination—

					s.	d.
Extry male .	.	.	.	.	2	3
Shuger .	.	.	.	.	1	0
Other extrys	.	.	.	.	1	9

Five shillings was an unusually large toll to levy in this way, but Stevie knew his man, and had little fear of failing to extract it; easy-going Dan would so certainly be loth to "get argufyin' and risin' ructions."

Next morning, Stevie started betimes on his two-mile walk. The raindrops had only just ceased pricking the wide, continuous puddle, which lent a Venetian aspect to the main street, and sounds of gurgling and dripping were audible all around, as if everything were talking over the late downpour. When Stevie faced towards the purple mountain range, in the direction of which lay Dan Farrell's, he saw the pale mists creeping along the ridges, and writhing up the ravines, and swirling in the curved hollows, and the air had the breath of autumnal chill that comes with rain in harvest time. Water gleamed greyly from the furrows of every little field that he passed, and he passed scores of them before he reached the river bridge, where he was within a few perches of his goal. He might have taken a shorter route, but it included a swampy patch and the passage of some stepping-stones, for which he considered the state of affairs "too soft altogether"; and he therefore kept upon comparatively dry land. The dryness was very comparative indeed all over Dan Farrell's little holding, which occupied the entrance to a winding green glen, where both stream and hillside curved suddenly, leaving a triangular bit of level ground. During the past night, however, this had undergone an abrupt change of contour, as the swollen river had flung an impetuous arm across it, islanding its apex and rejoining the main stream, turbid with melted clods and tangled with wisps of drowned green oats.

When Stevie came to the bridge, Dan Farrell himself was standing up to his knees in the soaked grain by the water's edge and thinking of his bad luck, without any presentiment that more was on its way. He was a tall, black-bearded man, and had been a gaunt and grizzled one ever since a virulent attack of rheumatism last spring had changed him from middle-aged to elderly in a few racking weeks. This illness had brought

Sarah Tighe, his sister's daughter, from her home in Athcrum to nurse him and manage his forlorn household, for Dan had lately been left a widower, and his four children were incapably small. Sarah was now calling to him from the door to the effect that he hadn't as much sense as little Bobby, or else he'd come in out of streeling through them oats, and they as wet as the waves of the say, unless maybe he'd a mind to have himself bawling for the next month with the pains in his bones. But Dan turned **a** bothered ear to her warnings, until she added—

"And if here isn't one of the young Grogans slingein' along over the bridge."

Then the recollection of his growing account at the shop started out from the misty background of his troubles, and took up a commanding position in the forefront. He cast a glance of listless despondency on the flooded field and turbulent river, and began to walk slowly up the plashy furrow towards his house, set in motion by a vague sense that it was more fitting for him than for his niece to receive young Grogan. By the time he reached the door, Stevie was already there talking to Sarah, a plump young woman, whose colouring suggested an autumn hedge-row, with gleams of ruddy berries and black, and warm brown leaves. She was naturally conversational and vivacious, but it may be feared that her consciousness of Brian Mahony inside there disapproving of the colloquy led her to carry it on with increased animation. Had nobody been by to mind, Mr Stephen Grogan might have received a welcome more in accordance with Sarah's own private opinion of him, which was low. When her uncle came up, she stood demurely aside, and waited while his health was inquired after and the weather bewailed. Then Stevie asked—

"And what way was the fair a' Tuesday?"

"As bad as anythin' at all," said Dan, "onless you was to be payin' the dalers to take your bastes off you for a complimint."

"But you're after selling a couple?" said Stevie.

"Och, did I—and what's four pound ten to git for a grand little heifer, and she a rael dexter, if you was to be tired swearin' agin it? Worth three times the money she'd ha' been to me, if I could ha' held on to her a sixmonth longer."

"Sure, now, it's you farmers that are the

rich people, makin' nothin' of pound notes at that rate," said Stevie, laughing with a sort of uneasy jocularity. Dan knew quite well what was coming, before the other went on, "So as I was passin' this way, I just looked in wid our bit of account, Misther Farrell; it's been runnin' this good while now."

"Ay, bedad," Dan assented dejectedly, "will you be steppin' inside?"

Inside reigned a brownish twilight, and the corners were all rounded off with smoke-haze. One of them was occupied by Brian Mahony, a neighbour of the Farrells, who, since Dan's illness, had often come in to lend him a hand. This morning he had undertaken the repairs of a turf-creel. He was a powerful-looking young man, with a shock of chestnut hair and tawny tufts and frills about his face, which just then wore a glum expression, mis-liking the entrance of Stevie Grogan. His dissatisfaction caused him to appear deeply absorbed in his task, and to discuss it with the little Farrells, who stood around to watch his splicing and weaving. They were unsus-pectingly flattered by his unusual disposition to consult them, and they favoured him with much criticism and advice.

"Sit you down, man, and warm yourself," said Dan, taking the glazy blue paper which young Grogan had extracted from a thin pocket-book bound in black American cloth, and tied round with frayed strings of pink tape. "I'm afeard we haven't e'en a sup of anythin' in the house."

As Stevie seated himself near the circle of glowing sods, Dan carried his bill over to the window, that the light of its one deep-set pane might assist his somewhat feeble scholarship in spelling out the items. Many of them baffled him completely, but the grand total of one pound five shillings appeared with cruel distinctness, and caused him serious dismay. He had been prepared for a sum that would make a very large hole in one of his few precious notes, and even this prospect was grievous. But the demand for a whole note, body and bones, and some silver too, came as an unexpected stroke. His hands shook as he held the paper to the light, obscured by the leaves of a straggling geranium plant, and he felt bitterly convinced that he was being cheated. Manners, however, would not permit him to enter any protest beyond saying to his niece—

"Musha, Sally, it's a terrible sight of sugar you seem to ha' been usin'."

Upon this Stevie of course said—

"And I'm sure *she* doesn't want it, any-way,"—smirking gallantly at Sarah, who had sat down in the adjacent chimney-corner and taken up her strip of lace-work.

"Won'erful fine talk you have," said Sarah.

"And divil a word but the truth, talkin' of you," rejoined Stevie, sidling a little nearer to her along his rickety-legged bench.

Sarah replied by making a threatening demonstration with her needle, which caused her frail thread to snap.

"There now, you have it broke on me," she said, "and sorra the bit of you's worth the throuble of tyin' a knot."

"Ah now, don't say so, Miss Tighe," Stevie said insinuatingly. "That's an iligant little pattron you have been doin', oncommon tasty. We have some thread-lace edgin' at our place that I declare isn't a ha'porth better, and it comes to as much as thruppence a yard." He intended the highest compliment, but did only plunge himself the deeper into the depths of her disfavour by thus evening her delicate point to his coarse, machine-made wares. She chose, however, for the time being, to dissemble her wrath against him, because she was angrier with Brian Mahony for his persistence in evidently ignoring her flirtation, and keeping up an unconcerned chatter addressed to the children. So she accepted Stevie's offer to join the broken thread for her, and was coquettishly derisive of his clumsy-fingered failures, with much tittering and ostentatious enjoyment of the situation ; and, in like manner, Brian worked away at the ragged-rimmed creel, and only desisted occasionally to scuffle sportively with Jimmy or Biddy for the possession of a long supple osier. Nobody could suppose him to care a thraneen what Sarah and the chap from Grogan's found so amusing. He had something else to do than to be botherin' his head about them.

Meanwhile the master of the house was performing his part—a sad one—in the small drama. He lifted a brown earthenware teapot out of its niche in the mud wall projecting beside the hearth. Its removal discovered the opening of another recess, whence he drew a rough deal box with a broken lid. In this the Farrells apparently stored miscellaneous valuables, for it contained a little roll of bank-notes, a grey flannel bag with silver in it, an old prayer-book that had belonged to Mrs Farrell, some spools of cotton, and so forth. Dan slowly peeled off one of the begrimed Munster notes, and, pre-occupied with regretful calculations, he forgot the shillings which were due, and restored box and teapot to their places. Then he laid down the note on the window-seat, spread out the bluish bill beside it, and stood smoothing both bits of paper with the palm of his hand.

"There's that," he said.

"Sure, I'll be signin' the resate," said Stevie, jumping up with alacrity, and producing his shiny black pocket-book and red chalk pencil. But he came to a pause as he noticed the absence of the silver. He looked interrogatively at Dan. The man's careworn, broken-down aspect, his lined face and tattered garments gave his creditor a conscience-stricken twinge, and for an instant suggested the possibility of renouncing that toll. Stevie, how-ever, quickly ascertained that this was too much to expect from himself; the sum would come in just then too handily to be forgone, and he com-promised the matter by resolving to see that the

Farrells were let off easily in their next account.
Future generosity is always easier than present
justice, especially when the postponed virtue can
be practised at somebody else's expense.   So—

"There was thim five shillin's comin' to us,"
said Stevie, continuing to look at Dan.

"Och, murder, tub be sure there was.   It's
meself's the gaby," said Dan disconcertedly;
and he went towards the niche to rectify his
blunder, but he was interrupted by his niece.

"Sure I'll fetch it out, Uncle Dan," she said.
"It's throublesome for you to be stoopin'."   Mr
Grogan can be puttin' his name on the
account."

She fumbled for a few moments in the box,
and came over to the window with a large
silver coin in her hand.   It was a crown-piece,
which, although it bore the stamp of the fourth
George, still retained its sturdy thickness and
bold outlines unimpaired, as if it had changed
owners slowly.   Around this she was wrapping
a bit of crumpled, thin paper, perceiving which
her uncle said—

"Sure, girl alive, I've got the note here right
enough."

"But it's my belief 'twas the dirtiest one you
had that you sorted out," replied Sarah

promptly. "Now *I*'ve found him a dacint clane one; and I'm sure you'd a dale liefer be takin' it wid you, Mr Grogan?"

"'Deed you may depind upon that, Miss Tighe," Stevie said, with an elated smirk; "and hard-set I'll be to part wid it, when I consider how you put yourself about to be pickin' and choosin' for me."

Here Brian Mahony abruptly threw down his creel and flung out of the house, with a scowl which did not escape Sarah's observation. It did not please her, somehow, any better than his previous air of unconcern, whence we may infer that her mood was capricious and contrary. Stevie Grogan, at any rate, presently had reason to think it so, and a flatness and tartness came over the conversation, not inviting him to prolong his visit. After three snubs—

"The day's darkenin' again," he said, "and I'll be getting along afore there's another plump of rain." He took leave of Dan, who was reflecting sorrowfully how much poorer a man the last half-hour had made him, and went to the door, accompanied by Sarah. "Bedad!" he said, glancing around, "I think the sthrame looks to have quieted itself a goodish bit. I might be steppin' across them stones, it saves better than a mile when you get into the bog over yonder."

It is possible that Stevie was determined to adopt this course less by the aspect of the river than by a glimpse which he at that moment had had of Brian lounging moodily upon the bridge where he must otherwise pass. But if that were the case, his plan failed of its purpose. For as he walked through the tangled oats followed by Sarah, who had bethought her of a message to give him for her mother, Brian espied them, and immediately descended from the bridge and made for the ford along the river's bank. He could not resist the spell which drew him to every opportunity of tormenting himself by witnessing what his jealous mind regarded as Sarah's marked pre-ference for young Grogan, and he sped so recklessly, stumbling and tripping over wisps of weeds and grass, that he reached the stepping-stones just as the others did.

On this occasion, however, his feelings were not to be harrowed by the display of much senti-ment or facetiousness at leave-taking, as it was drowned in a sudden burst of rain, which made Sarah pull her fringed shawl into deep eaves over her face, and gasp out with ducked head—

"Och, mercy on us, here's polthogues — I must run for me life, and you'd best step out, Stevie Grogan, or you'll be bogged entirely before you get home."

Thus exhorted, Stevie began hurriedly to stride from stone to stone. In one hand he held the shiny pocket-book, and with the other he clutched the brim of his black felt hat, which a rising gust momentarily threatened to whisk away. He was nearly half over, when the wind came swooping past in a furious flurry, and at the same time a thicker coil of the brown river-water broke on the stones, making one on which he had just set his foot wobble violently. The consequence was that he stumbled badly, only keeping his balance by a head-long plunge forward with outspread arms; and not till he had floundered on to the opposite bank did he perceive that his hat and book were both missing. His hat, after a high-whirled flight, lit on the rapid stream, and went skimming down it without let or hindrance, while his more precious book described a parabolic curve in the air, and dropped into the water near the place where Brian and Sarah stood. For a moment it lay on the surface, and Brian, leaning over at a dangerous angle, tried to reach it with his long osier rod. Upon which Sarah, gripping him by the arm, pulled him back with all her might, saying in an agonised tone:

"Och, goodness gracious, man, get out of that, and let it be!" But even as she spoke, the black cover, weighed down, no doubt, by the filched crown-piece, sunk out of sight and was no more seen. A few seconds later, however, the rough brown eddies a little lower down became strewn with small flecks whiter than the creamy foam. Evidently the strings and covers had collapsed, and let their frail contents go to wrack.

"Sure it's every bit of it flitthered into laves," said Sarah, releasing Brian's arm; "niver sight nor light of it he'll get the chance to lay eyes on agin, note or no note." The tone in which she announced this fact was both relieved and triumphant. As for the owner of that perishing property, he stood on the opposite bank, bare-headed in the pelting rain, discontented and woe-begone, an object to move pity. But Sarah added: "And the divil's cure to him, the thievin' slieveen. We've got the resate off him all right any way."

K

Brian, on the contrary, now took off his own limp cloth cap, crumpled it round a great shingle stone for ballast, and flung it across to Stevie.

"Clap that on your head, and be leggin' it home wid you, if you'll take my advice," he shouted against the wind; "you'll get nothin', unless it's your death of could, standin' there in the rain. Belike we might be some odd chance get the five shillin' piece at the bottom, when the river goes down, but them bits of papers is past prayin' for intirely." This seemed obvious even to the unwillingly convinced Stevie, and he started dolefully through the driving rain, half-blinded by it and the descending peak of Brian's too roomy cap. The others raced home under much less trying circumstances, and were speedily sheltered beneath Dan Farrell's thatch.

Sarah took her strip of lace-work, and sat down with it in the brighter patch by the window. She was filling in the centre of a fantastic blossom with a pattern which seemed to have been suggested by the dewy web of some long-legged spinner hitched from blade point to point. Brian Mahony fetched his creel and osiers out of the corner, and stood opposite to her, busy with his coarse weaving. Now and then he looked at her complacently as she stooped over her fine stitches, and for some time neither of them spoke. At last Brian said—

"That was a fine fright I'm after giving you down there, Sarah. You have the sleeve nearly rieved out of my ould coat. Was it dhrowndin' meself you thought I'd be that you took such a hould of me?"

"Dhrowndin' himself? Frightenin' me? Musha good gracious, what talk has the man out of him at all?" Sarah said with shrill ejaculation. "Bedad, if that was all that ailed the likes of you, I'd ha' had somethin' better to be at than throublin' myself to interfere wid you. But afeared I was that you'd be hookin' that chap's ould book ashore on us; thryin' your best you were to do that fool's thrick."

"And what for wouldn't I be saving it if I could?" said Brian, partly consoled for the unflattering explanation of his solicitude by the animosity of her tone when she mentioned that chap; "sure, onst the money was ped away, you were nothin' the better for it goin' to loss."

"That's all you know about it," said Sarah, with mysterious glee. She glanced round to see whether her uncle by the hearth were listening, and as he appeared to be half-asleep, she went on in a lower tone: "Why, look here, Brian — sure that grand clane pound-note I let on to be sortin' out for him, ne'er a note it was at all, but just an ould bit of the silver-paper pattron I had workin' me lace from; when it's crumpled up and creased like, it looks the very moral of one, and the great gomeral stuck it into his book widout takin' the throuble of unfoldin' it, be good luck."

"And what at all did you do that for?" asked Brian after a puzzled pause.

"What for?" said Sarah, "sure in the first beginnin' of it 'twas just to be risin' a laugh on him; that was all the notion I had. It come in me head when I was lookin' for the shillin's, and seen the thin paper there. But afterwards, when he tuk and put it up widout mindin', thinks I to myself, I'll ha' given him a good long thramp over it anyway; it's back he'll be thrapesin' to-morra or next day to get the right one, in a fine fantigue. But now when he's slung the whole affair into the wather, so as nobody'll be the wiser what was in th' ould pocket-book and what wasn't, that's the greatest chance could ha' happened,

and we wid the resate signed and all, the way
he can't say a word agin us. It's as good as
a pound saved to me uncle, poor man, that's
annoyed enough wid his bit of harvest ruinated
and everythin'. And you doin' your endeavours
to destroy it all wid fishin' the book out;
small blame to me if I'd pulled the fool's
arm off of you, let alone your ould sleeve."

"It was no thing to go do," said Brian
gruffly, "to be playin' them sort of thricks."

"Sorra the ha'porth of harm was there in
it," Sarah replied airily; "and considerin' that
whatever he got's swallied up in the river,
'twould ha' been a cruel pity if we'd gave
him anythin' betther."

"You'd a right to be sendin' him the rael
note now," said Brian with decision.

"Saints above! Whethen now, I hope
you'll get your health until I do," said Sarah,
with a shrillness subdued by her uncle's
proximity. "That'd be a nice piece of
foolery. Why, you sthookawn, the young
slieveen's no worse off this minute than he
would ha' been if I was after givin' him a
five-pound note to drop out of his hand."

"You got the resate off of him for nothin'
at all," said Brian; "he's never been ped.

And the river makes no differ. How would it, when he hadn't anythin' of yours to lose in it?"

"That's just what I'm sayin'. It makes no odds to him; he'd ha' lost it whether or no. And for the matther of that, he's been ped times and again for anythin' Uncle Dan ever got from them, poor man; for them Grogans are notorious thieves, as everybody well knows. Me sister was tellin' us the other day, they charge three shillin's a pound for tay that's on'y eighteen-pence in Dublin. It's a charity* to let them have a taste of chatin' for themselves. Not that we're chatin' them at all at all, it so happens."

Brian listened quite unimpressed, having no turn for casuistry. He now condescended, however, to urge an objection based upon the expedient.

"And what'll your uncle say to it, when he finds he's got a pound too much?"

"I was thinkin' of that," said Sarah, nowise disconcerted. "Belike I could persuade him he miscounted them at the fair. But I dare say 'twould be better if I just slipt one off the roll, and kep' it to get odds and ends of things wid for him, accordin' as they would be wanted, and never let on about it. Och, no fear, but I'll conthrive one way or the other."

"Ay, bedad; it seems to me that you're great at conthrivin' and schemin'," said Brian bitterly. "I've as good a mind as ever I had in me life to tell him the whole affair."

"And if you offer to do such a thing on me, you ould clashbag, you!" Sarah said in a furious whisper, "sorra a word I'll spake to you agin as long as I live in the world."

"Faix, then, perhaps I won't be throublin' meself to ax you in a hurry," retorted Brian, "when the on'y talk people has out of them is tellin' lies and makin' fools of everybody. My notion is, the fewer words they spake to you, the luckier you'll be."

"Plase yourself, and you'll plase me," said Sarah, with an assumption of calm indiffer- ence, which would have been more successfully achieved if she had not flushed to the scarlet of a frost-nipt brier leaf, besides adding incon- sistently, "I'd liefer hear the pigs gruntin' in the ould stye than to be listenin' to some people gabbin' and blatherin'."

"And plenty good enough company they are, too, poor bastes, for the likes of some I could name — and long sorry I'd be to stop anywheres I wasn't wanted, wastin' me time mendin' things, and gettin' imperance for it—

and one while it 'll be afore you 'll have raison to complain of me disturbin' you," said Brian, whose wrath had flared up even more ruddily than hers. And thereupon he bolted away into the rain, without waiting to borrow the loan of Dan's hat. At which Sarah through all her huff, stood somewhat aghast, knowing that for a man to go out of doors bareheaded argues no ordinary perturbation of spirit.

After this there were many more wet days, and a few golden fine ones, and the harvest was got in one way or the other, and the winter came, and Sarah Tighe went home to live with her family at Athcrum, and finished her fine lace border. But she and Brian did not meet again. At last, one bright, frosty morning, not long before Christmas, they ran against each other coming round the corner of the row in which the little post-office stands. Sarah was so startled that for a moment or two she halted, irresolute, ere she recollected that it behoved her to flounce past him with up-tilted chin. She was just proceeding to do so, when he twitched her shawl, and said, in an expostulatory tone—

"Och now, Sarah, is it cross wid me ye 're goin' to be all this time?"

"It isn't me that 's cross wid anybody at

all," said Sarah, subsiding lamentably from her dignified attitude.

"Sure then," said Brian, " I was on'y wantin' to tell you what I 've done about that pound-note was owin' to the Grogans. Sooner than that you 'd have anythin'—anythin' quare-like on your conscience, I 've saved up, and sent it to th' ould miscreant in a letter. So it can't come agin you now anyway. I 'm just after postin' it this minute."

"Och, murdher! and are you so?" said Sarah, with an accent of the keenest regret. "And weren't you the gomeral to not tell me that last week?"

"And I on'y droppin' it in the letter-box this instiant of time?" said Brian. "But at all events, what differ 'd that have made?"

"Differ enough," said Sarah ruefully. "You see, the fact of the matter was, when I come to considher, I didn't know but the ould naygur Grogan had a right to that pound-note after all; so last week, when I sold me flounce of deep lace for thirty shillin's, I got an order, and put it in a cover, and sent it to ould Natty himself. I wasn't goin' to let that young thief of the world, Stevie, be layin' one of his greasy fingers on it, anyhow; and even so I thought badly enough of postin' it away. For now the winter's comin' on us, there was a dale of things I'd liefer ha' done wid it."

"Begorra, that's the very same way it was wid me just now," said Brian.

"Maybe the post-mistress'd give it back to you, if you thried," suggested Sarah. "She couldn't hardly ha' done anythin' wid the letters yet."

"Sorra a thry I'll thry," said Brian, with decision. "Sure I wasn't manin' to say that I begrudged it e'er a bit, Sally, when it was settin' things straight for you, acushla."

"Ah, but to think of payin' them twyste over —that's what distresses me," said Sarah, who did not, however, look inconsolable. "'Deed, now, we managed it finely, Brian; I'm afeard that you and I are a great pair of fools."

But Brian replied with complacent promptitude, "True for you, then, Sally, machree; that's just the way it is. Fools we are, very belike, and a pair we are for sartin. Och now, honey, be aisy; sure 'twas yourself said it. And maybe we'll do all as well as if we'd had more wit. It's continted I am, anyway. Ay, bedad, a pair of fools—but them Grogans are welcome to their couple of pounds."

M'NEILLS' TIGER-SHEEP

M'NEILLS' TIGER-SHEEP

THE feud between the Timothy O'Farrells and Neil M'Neills at Meenaclure was not of very long standing, for the dowager Mrs O'Farrell and the elder Mrs M'Neill, who had been by no means young when it began, were still to the fore, and not yet even considered to have attained "a great ould age intirely." This seems a mere mushroom-growth compared with some of our family quarrels, which have been handed down from father to son through so many generations that everybody regards them as a part of the established order of things in the world of their parish. Still, to the younger people, who had been but children at its birth, it seemed to have lasted a long while, and their juniors would have found a different state of affairs almost unthinkable. For them the origin of the enmity had already begun to loom dimly through a mist of tradition, which would tend as time went on to grow vaguer and falser, until at length nobody would be left who could give a clear account of what it was all about. So far, however, all the neighbours who were "any age to speak of" knew the rights of the case well enough. And this is what had happened.

It was a cloudless midsummer evening, perhaps twenty years back—nobody is over-particular about chronology at Meenaclure—and all the dogs and children were away out on the wild land towards the mountains, minding the sheep, to keep them from coming home and eating up the crops. From April to October that was every year their occupation, and a very engrossing one they found it. For the scraggy little sheep of the district are endowed with an appetite for green food worthy of any locust, added to a cleverness at taking fences that would discredit no hunter; and this makes them a constant peril to the painfully-tilled fields, whose produce they threaten like a sort of visibly-embodied blight. Luckily, it is one whose ravages can be averted by timely precautions; and therefore, as soon as potatoes are *kibbed*, and oats sown, the sheep are driven off to a discreet distance on the moors, whence they are prevented from returning by a strong cordon of wary mongrels and active spalpeens. The children of such places as Meenaclure find the sunnier half of the year a season of perpetual school-vacation, when the longest days are watched out to their last lingering glimmer among the tussocks and boulders, so that the morning seems to have begun ages and ages ago by the time one straggles home, three - parts asleep on one's feet, the flocks having already betaken themselves to completer repose, or, recognising the unattainability of young green oats, having set their nibbling mouths safely up the swarded hill-slopes. For that night the fields may lie secure from marauding trespassers.

On this particular day, however, owing to some remissness of the young M'Neills and their shrewd-visaged dog, who were all led away by the excitement of a rabbit-hunt, one of the sheep under their charge successfully eluded observation, and broke through the line, with two comrades presently pattering after her. With a wiliness well masked by her expression of meek fatuity, she slunk along unseen in furzy folds of the broken ground, and late in the afternoon had arrived near the forbidden pastures. There she lurked furtively for a while, fully determined to hop

over the fence of Timothy O'Farrell's oatfield, ·
the very first moment that nobody seemed
to be about. This opportunity soon occurred,
as the O'Farrells' holding lies somewhat apart
in a slight hollow, which secludes it from the
little cabin-cluster standing a bit higher round
a curve in the long green glacis-like foot-
slope of Slieve Gowran.

Thus it came to pass that when Timothy
O'Farrell returned from turf-cutting on the
bog with his sister Margaret and his brothers
Hugh and Patrick, the first thing they noticed
was an object like a movable grey boulder
cropping up on the delicate sheeny surface
of their oat-patch. Whereupon: "Be the
powers of smoke," said Timothy, "if there
isn't them bastes in it agin."

"Three of them, no less," said Margaret.

"M'Neills', you may bet your brogues," said
Hugh.

"The divil doubt it," said Timothy. Patrick,
who was a youth of action rather than speech,
had already plunged head-foremost towards
the scene of the trespass.

There were several reasons why doubts of
the M'Neills' responsibility in the matter should
be relegated to the divil. In the first place,

the M'Neills owned more sheep than anybody
else at Meenaclure, whereas the O'Farrells
owned none; and secondly, the O'Farrells
had sown an unusually extensive patch of
oats, while the M'Neills had planted potatoes
only. The tendencies of this situation are
obvious. Again, the O'Farrells had more
than once before undergone the like inroads,
and on these occasions Neil M'Neill had not,
Timothy considered, shown by any means
an adequate amount of penitence. "Bedad,
now," Timothy reported to his family, "he
was cool enough over it. Maybe it's *his*
notion of fine farmin' to graze his bastes on
other people's growin' crops." A deep-rooted
sentiment of respect, however, restrained him
from uttering these sarcasms in public. For
Timothy, though the head and father of a
family, had seen not many more than a
score of harvests; and Neil, a dozen years
his senior, enjoyed a high reputation among
the neighbours as a very knowledgable man
altogether. After the second incursion, it is
true, Timothy's wrath had so far overcrowed
his awe as to make him "up and tell" Neil
M'Neill that "if he didn't mind his ould shows
of sheep himself, he'd be apt to find some-

L

body that'd do it in a way he mightn't
like." Still, the affair went no farther, and
Timothy had soon reverted to his customary
attitude of amicable veneration. But at this
third repetition of the offence his anger could
not be expected to subside so harmlessly.

Pat's shouts and flourishing gallop speedily
routed the conscious-stricken sheep, and two of
them whisked up the hillside like thistledown
on a brisk breeze; but the third, who was the
ringleader, leaped the fence with so little judg-
ment that she came floundering against Timothy,
who grasped her dexterously by the hind-legs.

Now, to catch a Slieve Gowran sheep alive
in the open is a rare and difficult feat—pro-
verbially impossible, indeed, at Meenaclure;
but Timothy and his brethren were at a loss
how they should best turn this achievement
of it to account. They felt that simply to let
the creature go again would be a flat and
unprofitable result, yet what else could they
do with it? While they pondered, and their
captive impotently wriggled, Hugh suddenly
had an inspiration. It came to him at the
sight of two large black pots, which stood
beside a smouldering fire against the white
end-wall of their little house. To an unen-

lightened observer, they might have suggested some gipsy encampment, but Hugh knew they betokened that his mother had been dyeing her yarn. The Widow O'Farrell was a great spinner, and a large part of the wool shorn in the parish travelled over her whirring wheel on its way to Fergus the weaver's loom. A few old sacks lying near the fire had contained the ingredients which she used according to an immemorial recipe. From the mottled grey lichen, *crottal*, which clothes our boulders with hues strangely like those of the fleeces browsing among them, she extracted a warm tawny brown; a flaky mass of the rusty black turf-soot supplied her with a strong yellow, and the dull-red bog-ore boiled paradoxically into black.

"Be aisy, will you, you little thief of the mischief," Hugh said to the sheep. "M'Neills' she is, sure enough; there's the mark. Musha, lads, let's give her a dab or so of what's left in the ould pots. 'Twould improve her apparance finely."

"Ay would it," said Timothy. "She's an unnathural ugly objic' of a crathur the way she is now. Bedad, they've a couple of barrels desthroyed on us."

" A few odd sthrakes of the black and yella 'd
make her look iligant," said Hugh. "Do you take
a hould of her, Tim. Och, man, don't let her
away, but lift her aisy. Maggie, did you see e'er a
sign of the stick they had stirring the stuff wid ?
But it's apt to be cool enough agin now."

" Ah, boys dear, but it's ragin' mad M'Neills
'll be if you go for to do such a thing,"
Margaret said, half-scared, and blundering in
her flurry on a wrong note, as she at once
perceived. For her brothers promptly re-
sponded in a sort of fugal movement—

" And sure who's purvintin' of them? They're
welcome, bedad, them, or the likes of them. Is
it ragin' ? Maybe it's raison they'll have before
they're a great while oulder, musha Moyah."
And they proceeded with all the greater en-
thusiasm to carry out their design, which became
more ambitiously elaborate in the course of
execution.

Early next morning, while the mountain-
shadow still threw a purple cloak over the steep
fields of Meenaclure, where all the dewdrops
were ready to twinkle as soon as a ray reached
them, and when Mrs Neil M'Neill was preparing
breakfast, which at this short-coming summer
season consisted chiefly of Indian meal, her eldest

daughter ran in to her with news. There was somethin', Molly said, leppin' about in the pig-stye. Now, the M'Neills' stye just then stood empty, in the interval between the despatch of their last lean fat pig to Letterkenny fair and the hoped-for fall in the market-price of the wee springy which was to replace him. So Mrs Neil said, "Och, blathers, child alive, what would there be in it at all?"

"But it's rustlin' in the straw,—I heard it, —and duntin' the door wid its head like," Molly persisted.

"Sure then, run and see what it is, honey," said her mother, who was pre-occupied with a critical stage of her porridge; and a piece of practical business on hand generally disposes us to adopt a sceptical attitude towards marvels. "Maybe one of the hins might have fluttered into it; but there's apter to not be anythin'."

Molly, whose mood was not enterprising, reinforced her courage with the company of Judy and Thady before she went to investigate; and a minute afterwards she came rushing back uttering terrified lamentations, whereof the burden seemed to be, "It's a tiger-sheep." Her report could no longer be disregarded, and the rest of the family were presently grouped round the low wall of the little lean-to shed, which did really contain an inmate of extraordinary aspect. Its form was that of a newly-shorn sheep, long-legged and lank-bodied like others of its race, but in colouring altogether exceptional. Boldly marked stripes of black and tawny yellow alternated all over it, with a brilliant symmetry not surpassed by the natural history chromograph which flamed on the wall of Rathflesk National School, and which now recurred to little Molly's mind in conjunction with the fact that the wearer of the striated skin "was a cruel, savage, wicked baste, that would be swallyin' all before it," whereupon she had shrieked "Tiger-sheep!" and fled from ravening jaws.

Her parents and grandparents, on the contrary, stood and surveyed the phenomenon with almost unutterable wrath. Traces of a human hand in its production were plain enough, for the beast had been fastened into the stye by a rope round her neck, which was further ornamented with long bracken-fronds and tufts of curiously-coloured wool, studiously grotesque. In fact, had she been mercilessly endowed with "the giftie," she would no doubt have suffered from a mortification as acute as was that of her owners, instead of trotting off quite satisfied, when once she was released and at liberty to resume her fastidious nibbling among the dewy tussocks.

"That's some divilment of the O'Farrells, and the back of me hand to the whole of them!" said Neil M'Neill, with clenched eyebrows. "Themselves and their blamed impidence, and their stinkin' brashes! The ould woman's niver done boilin' them up for her wool. It's slung about her head I wish they were, sooner than to be used for misthratin' other people's dacint bastes."

"'Deed now, thrue for you," said his mother. "Sure wasn't she tellin' me herself yesterday evenin' she'd been busy all day gettin' her yarn dyed, agin she would be knittin' the boys their socks? Gad'rin' the sut she said she was this good while. That's the way they done it— och, the vagabones!"

"It's a bad job," said old Joe M'Neill, shaking his despondent white head.

"I wouldn't ever ha' thought it of them," said Mrs Neil. "On'y them boys is that terrible wild; goodness forgive them, there's no demented notion they mayn't take into their heads. But what at all could we do for the misfort'nit crather? Sure it's distressful to see her goin' about that scandalous figure. I can't abide the sight of her."

Our bogland dyes, however, are very fast, and for many a day that summer Mrs Neil had to endure the apparition of the O'Farrells' victim, who of course became a painfully conspicuous object on the hillside, where she roamed blissfully unaware of how her owners' eyes followed her with gloomy resentment, and of how their neighbours' children, catching up Molly's cry, shouted one to another derisively, "Och, look at M'Neills' tiger-sheep!" But long and long after the parti-coloured fleece had vanished for good and all, the effects of the outrage continued to make themselves felt in the social life of Meenaclure, where it must be owned that the inhabitants are rather prone to keep their grudges in the same time-proof wallet with their gratitudes. And the grudges, somehow, often seem to lie atop. In this case, moreover, the injury had an especial bitterness, because the M'Neills came of an old sheep - keeping class, whose little flock was an inheritance handed down, dwindling, through many generations, and whose main interests and activities had time out of mind turned upon wool, so that everything connected with it had acquired in their eyes the peculiar sanctity with which we often invest the materials and implements belonging to our own craft. A chimney-sweep has probably some feeling of disinterested regard for his bags and brushes. Accordingly, sheep were to them a serious, almost solemn subject, altogether unsuitable for a practical joke; and an insult offered to them was felt to strike at the honour of the family. Small blame to them, therefore, if, as the neighbours said, they were ragin' mad entirely, and turned a deaf ear to all pacific overtures.

The O'Farrells, to do them justice, admitted upon reflection that they had maybe gone a little beyond the beyonds, and were disposed to be apologetic and conciliatory. But when old Mrs O'Farrell, one day meeting the two smallest M'Neills on the road, presented each of them with a pale brown egg, which she had just found in the nest of her speckled hen away down beside the river, the result merely was that her gifts were smashed into an impromptu omelet before the M'Neills' door, by the direction of the master of the house, who only wished the ould sinner had been there herself to see the way he'd serve that, or anythin' else she'd have the impidence to be sendin' into his place. And later on, when the feathery gold of the O'Farrells' oatfield had been bound in stooks, and the hobblede-hoy Pat was despatched to inquire whether the M'Neills might be wantin' e'er a thrifle of straw after the thrashin' for darnin' their bit of thatch, the polite attention elicited nothing except a peremptory injunction to "quit out of that."

In taking up this attitude, the M'Neills had at first the support of their neighbours' sym-pathy, public opinion being that it was no thing for the O'Farrells to go do. But as time went on, people began to add occasionally that sure maybe they didn't mean any such great harm after all, and that they were only young boyoes, without as much sense among the whole of them as would keep a duck waddling straight. What was the use of being so stiff over a trifle? These magnanimous sentiments were, no doubt, strengthened by the fact that in so small a community as Meenaclure a permanent breach between any two families could not but entail some incon-veniences upon all the rest. It was irksome,

for instance, to bear in mind throughout a
friendly chat that at the casual mention of a
neighbour's name the person you were talking
to would look "as bitter as sut" and freeze
into grim dumbness; or to have to consider,
should you wish for a loan of Widdy O'Farrell's
market-basket, that you must by no means
"let on" to her your intention of carrying
home in it Mrs M'Neill's grain of tea; or to
be called upon to choose between the company
of Neil M'Neill and Hugh O'Farrell on the
way home from the fair, because neither of
them, as the saying is, would look the same
side of the road as the other. Such obliga-
tions lay stumbling-blocks in our daily path,
and nip growths of good fellowship, and are
generally embarrassing and vexatious. However, Meenaclure had to put up with this state
of things for so many a long day that people
learned to include it unprotestingly among
their necessary evils.

Under these circumstances, it was of course
only in the nature of things that the little
M'Neills and O'Farrells, the smallest of whom
had not been born at the time of the quarrel,
should always put out their tongues at one
another whenever they met. They regarded

the salutation, indeed, as a sort of ceremonial observance, which could not be omitted without a sense of indecorum. Thus, one inclement autumn, when Patrick O'Farrell was no longer a hobbledehoy, but "as big a man as you'd meet goin' most roads," he went off to a *rabble*, that is, a hiring-fair, at Letterkenny, and took service for six months with a farmer away at Raphoe. On the day that he left Meenaclure, he happened, just as he was setting out, to meet Molly M'Neill, who had by this time grown into "a tall slip of a girl going on for sixteen," and they duly exchanged the customary greeting, Pat getting the better of her by at least half-an-inch of insult. But when he returned on a soft April evening, it chanced again that one of the first persons he fell in with was Molly. She was coming along between the newly-clad hedges of a narrow lane, and when he caught sight of her first he mistook her for his cousin, Norah O'Farrell, she looked so much taller than his recollections. But, on perceiving his error, he merely gave up his intention of saying, "Well, Norah, and how's yourself this great while?" and slunk past without making any demonstration whatever. Molly would hardly have noticed

it, indeed, as when she saw him coming she
began to minutely examine the buds on the
thorn-bushes, and did not lift an eyelash while
they were passing. ·Yet, as they went their
several ways, Pat felt that he had somehow
shirked a duty; and Molly, for her part, could
not shake off a sense of having failed in loyalty
to her family until she had relieved her conscience by announcing at home that she was
"just after meetin' that great *ugly*-lookin'
gomeral, Pat O'Farrell, slingein' down the
road below Widdy Byrne's."

The year which followed this spring was
one of bad seasons and hard fare at Meenaclure,
and towards the end of it Pat O'Farrell came
reluctantly to perceive that he could best
mend his own and his family's tattered fortunes
by emigrating to the States. His resolve,
though regretted by all his neighbours, except
of course the M'Neills, was considered sensible
enough; and at the "convoy" which assembled
according to custom to see him off on his
long journey the general purport of conversation was to the effect that, bedad, everybody'd
be missing poor Pat, but sure himself was
the fine clever boy wouldn't be any time
gettin' together the price of a little place

back again in the ould country. The M'Neills alone were of the opinion, expressed by Neil's mother, that "the only pity was the rest of the pack weren't goin' along wid Pat; unless, like enough, they'd be more than the people out in those parts could put up wid all at onst, the way they'd be landin' them back on us like a bundle of ould rubbish washin' up agin wid the tide."

But surprise was the universal feeling when, about six months later, it became known that Neil M'Neill's eldest child Molly had also made up her mind to cross over the water. Her own family were foremost among the wonderers; for Molly had always been considered rather excessively timid and quiet— certainly the very last girl in the parish whom one would have thought likely to make such a venture. They half believed that when it came to the point, "sorra a fut of her would go"; and they much more than half hoped so, notwithstanding that their rent had fallen into alarming arrears, and none of her brethren were old enough to help. Molly, however, actually went, amid lamentations and forebodings, both of her own and other people's, all alike unavailing to stop her.

Mrs Timothy O'Farrell said she'd be long sorry
to have a daughter of hers streeling off to the
ends of the earth. And I think that Molly's
mother *was* long sorry, poor soul, through
many a lonesome day and anxious night.

After these two departures, things at Meenaclure took their wonted course, a little more
sadly and dully perhaps than heretofore.
Communications from abroad came rarely and
scantily, for neither of the absentees had much
scholarship. Their sheep-herding summers had
greatly curtailed that, and it would have been
difficult to say whether Pat's or Molly's scrawls
were the briefer or obscurer. But not long
after Molly M'Neill had gone, one of Pat
O'Farrell's letters contained an important piece
of news—nothing less than that he was "just
about gettin' married." He did not go into
particulars about the match, merely describing
the future Mrs Pat as the "best little girl in
or out of Ireland," and opining that they
mightn't do too badly. His family were not
overjoyed at the event, which might be considered to presage a falling off in remittances;
and his mother was much cast down thereby,
her thoughts going to the tune of "my son
is my son till he gets him a wife." Still,

she was not so dispirited as to be past finding some solace in an innuendo ; and she
almost certainly designed one when she took
occasion to remark just outside the chapel
door, where she had been telling the neighbours her news : " But ah, sure, I don't mind
so long as he hasn't took up wid one of them
black-headed girls I never can abide the looks
of. And 'deed now there 's no fear of that.
Pat 's just the same notion as myself, I know
very well." For Mrs Neil M'Neill was standing well within earshot, and, as everybody
remembered, " there wasn't a fair hair on the
head of e'er a one of her childer." However,
Mrs Neil proved equal to the emergency,
and remarked, addressing Katty Byrne, that
" It was rael queer the sort of omadhawns
she 'd heard tell of some girls, who, belike,
knew no better, bein' content to take great
lumberin' louts of fellers, wid the ugly-coloured
hair on their heads like nothin' in the world
except a bit of new thatch before it would
be combed straight."

She spoke without any presentiment that
she would soon have to go through much the
same experience as old Mrs O'Farrell ; but
so it was. For a week or two later came a

letter from Molly stating that she was "just
after gettin' married." Her husband, who she
said was earning grand wages, bore the ob-
noxious name of O'Farrell, but there was
nothing strange in the coincidence, as the
district about Meenaclure abounds in Farrells
and Neills, with and without prefixes of O
and Mac; and it seemed only natural to suppose a similar state of things in New York.
Nobody could deny that there were plenty
of O'Farrells very dacint people. So Molly's
mother mourned in private over an event
which seemed to set a seal upon the separa-
tion between her daughter and herself; and
in public was well pleased and very proud,
laying great stress upon the fact that Molly
had sent the money-order just as usual,—
"Sorra a fear of little Molly forgettin' the
ould people at all,"—and serenely scorning
Mesdames O'Farrell's opinion that "when a
girl had to thravel off that far after a
husband, it was the quare crooked stick of a
one she'd be apt to pick up."

After this Meenaclure received no very
thrilling foreign news for about a twelvemonth. Then one fine Sunday, the Widdy
O'Farrell was to be seen sailing along Mass-

wards, with her head held extremely high in its stiff-frilled cap and dark blue hood, and with a swinging sweep of her black homespun skirt, which betrayed an exultant stride. All her family, indeed, wore a somewhat elated and consequential air, which most of her neighbours allowed to be justifiable when she explained that she had become the happy grandmother of her Pat's fine young son : the letter with the announcement had come last night. This was indeed promotion, for her son Tim's children were all girls. With the congratulations upon so auspicious an event even old Mrs M'Neill could mingle only subdued murmurs about brats taking after their fathers that weren't good for much, the dear knows. However, she had not long to wait for as good or better a right to strut chin in air, since it was with a great-grandmother's dignity that a few days later she could inform everybody of the arrival of Molly's boy. She would, I believe, have found it very hard to forgive Molly if the child had been merely a daughter.

This rivalry, as it were, between the estranged families in the matter of news from their non-resident members recurred with the same equipoised result on more than one similar occasion, and was extended even to less happy events. For instance, one time when Pat wrote in great distraction, and a wilder scrawl than usual, that the "three childer was dreadful bad wid the mumps, he doubted would they get over it," the next mail brought just such a report from Molly; which was rather awkward for her mother and grand-mother, who had been going about passing the remark that "when childer got proper mindin' they never took anythin' of the sort."

At length, however, when perhaps half-a-dozen years had gone by, the balance of good fortune dipped decidedly towards the O'Farrells. One autumn morning a letter came from Pat to say that he and his family were coming home. He had saved up a tidy little bit of money, and meant to try could he settle himself on a dacint little bit of land; at any rate he would get a sight of the ould place and the ould people. Great was the rejoicing of the O'Farrells. Whereas for the M'Neills at this time the meagre mail-bags contained no foreign letter, no letter at all, bad or good, let alone one fraught with such grand news. Molly's mother, it is true, dreamt two nights running that Molly had come home; but dreams are a sorry substitute for a letter, especially when everybody knows, and some people remind you, that they always go by contraries. So Mrs Neil fretted and foreboded, and had not the heart to be sarcastic, no matter how arrogantly the O'Farrells might comport themselves.

Then the autumn days shrivelled and shrank, and one morning in late November the word went round Meenaclure that the *Kaley* that evening would be up at Fergus the weaver's. This meeting-place was always popular, Fergus being a well-liked man, with a wide space round his hearth. And this night's conversazione promised to be particularly enjoyable, as it had leaked out that Dan Farrell and Mrs Keogh and Dinny O'Neill were concerned in what is at Meenaclure technically termed "a join," for the purpose of treating the kaleying company to cups of tea. In fact, the materials for that refreshment, done up in familiar purple paper parcels, lying on the window-seat, were obvious to everybody who came into the room, though to have seemed aware of them would have been a grave breach of manners. When all the company were mustered, and the fire was burning its brightest, Fergus might well look round his house with satisfaction, for so large an assembly seldom came together, and universal harmony seemed to prevail. This was not disturbed by the fact that several both of the Timothy O'Farrells and Neil M'Neills were present, as by this time everybody thoroughly understood the situation, and the neighbours arranged themselves as a matter of course in ways which precluded any awkward juxtapositions of persons "who weren't spakin'."

It was a showery evening, with a wafting to and fro of wide gusts, which made the Widdy O'Farrell wonder more than once as she sat on the form by the hearth, with the Widdy Byrne interposed buffer-wise between her and old Joe M'Neill. What she wondered was, whether her poor Pat might be apt to be crossin' over the say on such an ugly wild night. Just as Mrs Keogh, with an eye on the lid-bobbing kettle, was about to ask Fergus if he might happen to have e'er a drop of hot water he could spare her—that being the orthodox preface to tea-making on the occasion of a join — the house-door rattled violently, and opened with a fling. As nobody appeared at it, this was supposed to be simply the wind's freak, and Fergus said to Mick M'Murdo, who sat next to it, "Musha, lad, be givin' it a clap to wid your fut." But at that instant a voice was heard close outside, calling as if to another person a little farther off, "Molly, Molly, come along wid you; they're all here right enough, and I wouldn't be keepin' the door open on them." Whereupon there was a quick patter of approaching feet, followed by the entrance of two bundle-bearing figures. As they advanced into the flickering light, it showed that the figures were a man and a woman, and the bundles children; and in another moment there rose up recognising shrieks and shouts of "Pat" and "Molly," and then everybody rushed together tumultuously across a chasm of half-a-dozen years.

"They tould us below at Widdy Byrne's that we'd find yous all up here," said Pat O'Farrell, "so we left the baby there, and stepped along. Och, mother, it's younger you're grown instead of oulder, and that's a fac.'"

"And where's the wife, Paudyeen agra?" said Pat's mother; "or maybe she sted below wid the. child?"

"And where's himself, Molly jewel?" said Molly's mother. "Sure you didn't come your lone?"

"Why, here he is," said Molly. "Pat, man, wasn't you spakin' to me mother?"

"Och, whethen now, and is it Pat O'Farrell?" his mother-in-law said with a half-strangled gasp.

"And who else would it be at all at all, only Pat?" said Molly, as if propounding an unanswerable argument.

"Mercy be among us all—and you niver let on—och, you rogue of the world—you niver let on, Patsy avic, it was little Molly M'Neill you'd took up wid all the while," said his mother.

"Sure I was writin' to you all about her times and agin," Pat averred stoutly.

Perhaps things might have turned out differently if people had not been delighted and taken by surprise. But as it was, how could a feud be conducted with any propriety when Mrs Neil had unprotestingly been hugged by Pat O'Farrell, and when old Joe M'Neill and his wife and daughter were already worshipping a very fat small two-year-old girl, who unmistakably featured all the O'Farrells that ever walked? The thing was impossible.

For one moment, indeed, an unhappy resurrection seemed to be threatened. It was when everybody had got into a circle round the hearth, in expectation of the cups of tea, which were beginning to clatter in the back-ground, and when Pat O'Farrell, who was talking over old times with Neil M'Neill, suddenly gave his father-in-law a great thump on the back, exclaiming with a chuckle, "Och, man, and do you remimber your ould sheep that we got in the oats, and gave a coloured wash to? Faix, but she was the comical objec'—'the tiger-sheep,' the childer used to call her." Whereupon all the rest looked at one another with dismayed countenances, as if they had caught sight of something uncanny. But their alarm was needless. For Neil returned Pat's thump promptly with interest, and replied, "Haw, haw, haw! Bedad, and I do remimber her right well. Och now, man alive, I'll bet you me best brogues that wid all you've been behouldin' out there in the States you niver set eyes on e'er a baste'd aquil her for quareness—haw, haw, haw!" And the whole company took up the chorus, as if minded to make up on the spot all arrears of laughter owing on that long un-appreciated joke. Amid the sound of which I have reason to believe that there fled away from Meenaclure for ever the last haunting phantasm of the unchancy tiger-sheep.

THE SNAKES AND NORAH

THE SNAKES AND NORAH

THE Kennys' little farmstead was a somewhat amphibious one, occupying the
southern end of the isthmus which keeps
the Atlantic foam from riding into Lough
Fintragh, a small, dark-watered nook niched
in the shadow of steep mountain slopes.
Another murkier shadow brooded over it in
the opinion of the Kennys, who, like most
of their neighbours, at least half - believed
that its recesses harboured a monstrous in-
dweller. Their thin white house stood fronting the seashore, with a narrow grazing strip
behind, while their yard and sheds lay along
the dwindling isthmus, which becomes a mere
reef-like bar of boulders and shingle before
it again touches the mainland. In calm
weather Joe Kenny might see his unimposing
ricks reflected from ridge to butt, with gleams
of ochre and amber and gold in both salt
and fresh water; but in stormy times, which
came oftener, it might befall him to witness
a less pleasing spectacle of hay-wisps and
straw-stooks strewn bodily, floating and soak-

ing on the wasteful waves. So he was not
surprised to find that this had happened
when he walked out one December morning
after a wild night whose blustering had
mingled menace with his dreams. Despite
its close-meshed roping and thick fringe of
dangling stone weights, the more exposed
haystack had been seriously wrecked and
pillaged. "Och, bad cess to the ould win'
and its whillaballoos!" said Joe, as he surveyed the distorted outlines, and made a
rueful estimate of the damage. "If I got
the chance to slit its bastely bellows for it,
'twould be apt to keep its huffin' and puffin'
quiet for one while — it would so." This
was not, however, the limit of his losses.
Presently he stood looking vexedly over the
door of a half-roofed shed, which contained a
good deal of sea-water and weed ; also a
very small red calf, and a large jelly-fish.
The calf was drowned dead, but the jelly-
fish seemingly lived as much as usual.
"Eyah, get out wid you, you unnathural-
lookin' blob of a baste!" said Joe, giving
this unprofitable addition to his stock a
contumelious flick with his blackthorn.
"There's another good fifteen shillin's gone

on me.   I 'd never ha' thought 'twould ha'
tuk and slopped over the wall that way.
Sorra the bit of a Christmas box I 'll be
able to conthrive her this year, and that 's
a fac' ; and to-morra fair day and all—weary
on it ! "

" Her " was Rose O'Meara, Joe's sweetheart ;
and since he had long looked forward to the
opportunity of the Christmas gift as likely
to bring about a favourable crisis in his
courtship, the falling through of his plan
made him feel dejectedly out of humour, in
which unenjoyable mood he strolled on towards the pigstye.   Traces of the spent
storm lay all around him.   The tide had
receded some way, but the waves were fast by,
still hissing and seething, and flinging themselves down with hollow booms and thuds.
They had evidently been beating high against
the yard-wall, for all along it they had left
great masses of brown sea-wrack tossed in
bales and clumps, as if loaded out of a cart ;
and these were connected by trails of green
and black weed, skeleton branches, shells,
clotted froth, driftwood, and other debris, all
in an indescribable tangle.   As Joe stumped
through it, he trucks his foot sharply against

something hard, and nearly tripped up. When he recovered his balance, he saw that the obstruction was not the boulder which he had already execrated in haste. It was a wooden box. In much excitement Joe picked it up, and set it on the top of the wall for exacter scrutiny. The tides were constantly sweeping in with miscellaneous fringes on the Kennys' demesne, but seldom did they bring anything that might not be justly termed "quare ould rubbish." During all the course of Joe's life, and he was not in his first youth, no waif had been washed up so promising in appearance as this box. About ten inches square it was, and made of a fine grained dark wood, which seemed to have been very highly polished. The corners were clamped with bronze-like metal, elaborately wrought, and plates of the same inlaid the keyhole and hinges. So strong was the lock, that when he tried to wrench off the lid he seemed to have a solid block in his hands, and it shut so tightly that the lines of juncture were almost invisible. Its weight was considerable enough to increase his conviction that it held something very precious.

Joe's first impulse was to rush home with his prize, exhibit and examine it. Immediately afterwards, however, it flashed across him like an inspiration· that here was Rose's Christmas box; and upon this followed a more leisurely resolve to keep it a secret until he should present her with it intact on Christmas morning, still distant three whole days. This course would cost him the repression of much impatient curiosity, but it was recommended to him by a sense that it would enhance the value of the gift. He would be making over to Rose all the vague and wonderful possibilities of the treasure-trove, which in his imagination were more splendid than any better-defined object, as they loomed through a haze of unseen gold and jewels. Disappointment had scanty room among his forecasts. "Sure, I'd a right to give it to her just the way it is, wid anythin' at all inside it, for amn't I axin' her to take meself in a manner like that, whether good, bad, or indiff'rint comes of it?—on'y it's scarce as apt, worse luck, to be any great things as the full of a grand lookin' box is. But she might understand 'twas as much as to say I'd be wishful she had every chance of the best that I could git for her, the crathur, if it was all the gold and silver and diamonds that ever were dhrownded under the say-wather, and 'd never think to be lookin' to reckon them, no more than if they were so many handfuls of ould pebbles off of the strand." Thus reflected Joe, who had a vein of sentiment, which sometimes outran his powers of expression. And thereupon, leaving the box atop of the wall, he went to look after the pigs. He found them all surviving, though the storm had caused some dilapidations in their abode, which obliged him to do a little rough carpentry, and kept him hammering and thumping for several minutes. And when he returned to the place where he had left the box, the box was gone.

He searched wildly for it among the litter on both sides of the wall, and nowhere could it be seen. Yet at that hour what man or mortal was there abroad to have stirred it? Then he thought that the weeds looked wetter than they had been, and he said to himself that "one of them waves must ha' riz up permiscuous and swep' it off in a flurry while his back was turned;

and a fine gomeral he'd been to go lave it widin raich of such a thing happenin' it." So as no more satisfactory explanation was forthcoming, he turned homeward, empty-handed and crestfallen. But before he had taken many steps, he saw sitting under the lee of the yard-wall Tom O'Meara, Rose's brother, who was generally recognised to be courting Mary Kenny, Joe's youngest sister. The O'Mearas lived a good step beyond the other end of the isthmus, and Joe had begun to speculate what so early a visit might signify, when the greater wonder abruptly swallowed the less as he became aware that Tom had the twice-lost box in his hands.

"Look-a, Joe, at what I'm after findin'," he called jubilantly.

"Findin'? Musha moyah! that's fine talkin'," said Joe. "And where at all did you find it, then?"

"Where it was to be had," said Tom, promptly adjusting his tone to Joe's, which was offensive.

"Then it's sitting atop of our wall there it was," said Joe. "Whethen, now, some people has little enough to do that they can't keep their hands off meddlin' wid things

N

they find sittin' on other people's yard-walls."

"And suppose it was sittin' on anybody's ould wall," said Tom, "what else except a one of them rowlin' waves set it sittin' there wid itself, and it all dhreepin' wet out of the say? Be the same token it's quare if one person hasn't got as good a right to be liftin' it off as another. Troth and bedad, I'd somethin' betther to do than to be standin' star-gazin' at it all day, waitin' to ax lave of the likes of yous."

"I'll soon show you the sort of rowlin' wave there was, me man, if you don't throuble yourself to be handin' it over out of that, and I after pickin' it up this half-hour ago," said Joe, with furious irony.

"Come on wid you, come on!" Tom shouted, jumping to his feet with a general flourish of defiance. At this point the dispute bade fair to become an argument without words, and would probably have done so had it not been that the two young men were the brothers of their sisters. As it was, a sort of Roman-Sabine complication fettered and handcuffed them. "Divil a thing else I was intendin' to do wid it, but bring it straight ways in to your sister Mary," said Tom, "that you need go for to be risin' rows about the matter."

"It's for Rose's Christmas box; that's what I think bad of," said Joe.

"Let's halve it between the two of them, then, whatever it is," said Tom, feeling that a compromise was the utmost he could reasonably expect from circumstances.

And so it was arranged, rather weakly on Joe's part, he being the better man of the two, and well within his rights, if he had chosen to claim the box unconditionally. The joint presentation should take place, they agreed, on Christmas Eve, the next day but one, when Rose O'Meara would be visiting the Kennys; and then Tom departed whistling, with the pick he had come to borrow the loan of, while Joe consoled himself as best he could for this arbitrary subtraction of more than half the pleasure and romance from his morning's find.

Late on Christmas Eve, when the Kennys' kitchen was full of glancing firelight, and the widow Kenny, with her son and daughters and her guests, Tom and Rose O'Meara, had all had their tea, Joe and Tom were seen to often whisper and nudge one another, until at last Joe got up and produced the box from its secret hiding-place. But Tom hastened to forestall him as spokesman, placing considerable confidence in his own perspicacity and grace of diction. He said—

"See you here, Mary and Rose. This consarn's a prisint the two of us is after gettin' the two of yous—I mane it was Joe found it aquilly the same as me, that picked it up somethin' later. And it's he's givin' the whole of his half of the whole of it to Rose; but he's nothin' to say to the rest of it; and it's meself that's givin' Mary the half of the whole of the half—och no, botheration! it's the whole of the—it's the other whole half of it—"

"You've got it this time," Joe remarked in a sarcastic aside.

"—I'm givin' Mary. So that's the way of it, and when we've got the lid prized off for yous, you'll just have to regulate it between yous, accordin' to what there is inside."

"And if it's all the gold and diamonds in the riches of the world," said Joe, "you're kindly welcome to every grain of it, Rose jewel—ay, bedad, are you."

"To the one half of it," corrected Tom,

with emphasis. But his sister tapped him
with the pot-stick, and said, "Whisht, you big
omadhawn, whisht."

"It's a pity of such a thing to be knockin'
about and goin' to loss," said Mary, rubbin'
her finger on the embossed metal-work; "and
I wonder what's gone wid whatever crathur
owned it. Under the salt say he's very apt
to be lying this night—the Lord be good to
him!" The rustle of the waves climbing up
the shingle outside seemed to swell louder
as she spoke.

"For anythin' we can tell, he might be
takin' a look in at us through the windy
there this minute to see what we're doin' wid
it," said Joe.

Everybody's eyes turned towards the dark
little square of the window, and Mary left off
handling the box as suddenly as if it had
become red-hot.

"Oh, blathers!" said Tom. "Just raich me
the rippin'-chisel that's lyin' on the windy-stool,
Norah, and we'll soon thry what it is at all."

Norah, the elder sister, made a very long
arm, and secured the tool with as little
approximation as might be to the deep-set
panes. She had neither sweetheart nor Christ-

mas box, and was disposed to take a rather languid and cynical view of affairs.

"There's apt not to be any great things in it, I'm thinkin'," said the widow Kenny from her elbow-chair by the hearth. The truth was that she had been reflecting with some bitterness how not so many years since Joe would have "come flourishin' in to her wid any ould thrifle of rubbish he might ha' picked up outside," whereas now he had kept this valuable property silently in his possession for three days, for the purpose of bestowing it upon the O'Mearas' slip of a girl. Consequently, Joe's mother held aloof from the eager group round the table, and uttered disparaging predictions of the event. Tom and Mary did make a prudent attempt to fend off their collision with the disappointment which might emerge from the mists ahead by repeating, as the chisel wrestled with the stubborn hasps and springs, "Sure, all the while belike there's on'y some quare ould stuff in it, no good to anybody." Joe and Rose, on the contrary, chose to run under crowded sail towards the possible wreck of their hopes, and talked of sovereigns and bank-notes and jewels while the lid creaked and resisted.

But when at length it yielded with a final splinter, it disclosed what no one had anticipated—namely, nothing. The box was quite empty. Daintily lined with glossy satinwood, as if for the reception of something delicate and precious, but bare as the palm of your hand. There was not even so much vacant space as might have been expected, for the sides were disproportionately thick. Very blank faces exchanged notes with one another upon this result. Almost any contents, however inappropriate and worthless, would have been their "advantage to exclaim upon," and more tolerable for that reason than mere nullity, about which there was little to be said. Rose was the first to rally from the general mortification, observing with forced cheerfulness that "sure 'twould make an iligant sort of workbox, at all ivints, and 'twas maybe just as handy there bein' nothin' in it, because 'twould hould anythin' you plased." To which Mary rejoined, dejectedly refusing to philosophise, "Bedad, then, you may keep it yourself, girl alive, for the lid's every atom all smashed into smithereens."

The young people were not, however, with

one exception, in the mood for dwelling upon the dark side of things. Their depression caused by the collapse of the Christmas box was superficial, and soon passed away. When in course of the evening the two young men went out to feed the pigs, Rose and Mary accompanied them to the back door, where they all loitered so long that the patience waiting round the empty trough must have been sorely tried. Sounds of their talking and laughing came down the passage and were heard plainly in the kitchen, whence Mrs Kenny had slipped up her ladder stairs to say her rosary, so that Norah was for the time left quite alone. She was decidedly out of humour, albeit by no means on account of the others' rapid reverse of fortune. Rather, we may apprehend, she had viewed that incident as a not regrettable check to a tide of affairs which was unduly sweeping all manner of good luck her neighbours' way, and unjustly leaving her high and dry. This grudging spirit had forbidden her to appear interested in the examination of the box, but now she could satisfy without betraying her curiosity. As she drew her fingers aimlessly round its

smooth inner surface, there was a sudden
snap and jerk, and out slid a secret drawer,
which had been concealed by a false bottom.
It was filled with rose-pink wadding, amongst
which lay the coils of a long gold snake
necklace. She lifted it out amazedly, and
held it up in the firelight, with jewelled
head gleaming and enamelled scales, a far
finer piece of workmanship than she knew,
though the flash of brilliants and rubies
assured even her uninstructed eyes that she
had come on something of much value.

While she was still looking at it she heard
steps returning up the passage, and forthwith
tried hastily to replace it in the box. But
at a clumsy touch the drawer flew back into
its former invisibility, and her flurried fumbling
failed to press the lurking spring. Then, as
the steps came very near, she thrust her
ornament into her pocket, and moved away
from the table on which the box stood. In
doing so, she was conscious only of a proud
perversity which made her loth to be found
meddling with what she sullenly called "no
consarn of mine." Presently, however, other
motives for concealment grew clearer and
stronger. Of course, the longer she retained

it the more difficult would the restoring of it
be. Her crossness made it impossible for her
to imagine a joke as a natural explanation
of her conduct. Moreover, a covetous wish to
keep the beautiful thing for its own sake
sprang up, and had a swift growth. She said
to herself that "she didn't see why she need
have any call to be givin' it up, after all.
Wasn't she after findin' it in the quare little
slitherin' tray, and the rest of them wid no
more notion of it bein' there at all than ould
Sally the goat had? It might be lyin' where
it was till the world's end on'y for her? And
sure, for the matter of that, the ould box
itself was no more a belongin' of the lads
to give away than of any other body that
might ha' happened on it tossin' about the
shore. So if it wasn't theirs be rights, she
thought she'd be a fine fool to not keep
what she'd got." Sophistical arguments such
as these convinced her reason easily enough,
but her conscience was less amenable to them.
They were reinforced by some further considerations which possessed no ethical value
at all, and which she had the grace to be
ashamed of putting into clearly outlined
thoughts. She allowed herself to have only

a vague sense of grievance at the fact that
Rose and Mary had "presents, and people to
be makin' fools of them, and all manner,"
whereas none of these desirable things were
bestowed on her. Yet it formed a mental
atmosphere which made the prospect of yield-
ing up her discovery seem incongruous and
odious, in the same way that a bitter wind
blowing makes us loth to throw open our
doors and windows.

"Cock them up to be gettin' everythin'," she
said to herself, as she sat in a corner with
her hand in her pocket, and drew through
her fingers the cold, smooth coils, remembering how the gem-encrusted head had blazed
in the firelight. She wished that she could
venture to take it out and proudly display it
as her property ; but she was far from daring
to do so. On the contrary, she felt herself
laden with a guilty secret, and was presently
beset by all the misgivings, suspicions, and
surmises which infest people who carry about
such a burden. Whenever anyone went near
the box her heart thumped with terror lest
the drawer should be detected, and its rifled
condition somehow traced to her. Then she
trembled to think that the lads perhaps knew

all the time of the necklace's existence, and were just reserving it for a grand surprise; or she imagined herself letting it drop accidentally and being unable to account for her possession of it. These speculations so preoccupied her that she was obliged to explain her absent-mindedness by declaring herself "intirely disthracted wid the toothache"; upon which the condolences and sympathy of the others aggravated her uneasiness with remorseful gratitude. Her conscience nipped her shrewdly when Rose said, "Ah, the crathur, I'll run over to-morra early and bring you the bottle ould Matt Farren gev me mother; it's the grandest stuff at all for the toothache,"—Rose whom she was defrauding of a share in that golden marvel! At length she had resource to a plan which promised her temporary relief from urgent fears and self-reproaches. This was to hide away the necklace in some cranny of the rocks on the shore, where, if it should be rediscovered, nothing would implicate her in the matter. She said to herself, indeed, that they would have just as much chance of finding it there as in the mysterious drawer; but beneath that soothing reflection lay a resolve to minimise the chance by choosing the most unlikely chink possible. Since the evening was by this time far spent, and the O'Mearas had already taken leave, she knew that she must hurry to execute her design before Joe came in from seeing after the cattle, when the house would be shut up. So she slipped quietly out of doors.

It was a dark, gusty night, and the waves, still turbulent after their late uproar, were clattering noisily up the shingly ridges of the beach. As Norah ran along she could barely discern the glimmering of pale grey stones and white foam-crests. She kept on by the lough side of the isthmus, because the walking there was smoother, but when she thought she had come a safe distance she stopped, intending to cross over and seek a hiding-place for her spoil among a small chaos of weeded boulders. Looking for a moment athwart the black water, she saw a dim streak of light in the sky above it. The moon was glimpsing out of an eastern cloud-rift, and throwing down a meagre web of rays, which the unquiet dark surface caught fitfully and shredded into the broken coils of a writhing silver serpent. Perhaps it was this, or perhaps the golden snake-chain in her hands, that suggested the thing, but at any rate Norah suddenly bethought her of the *Piast*. For Lough Fintragh is haunted by the terror of one of these monsters, a huge and grisly worm, dwelling down in the shadowy end of the lake, where the water is said to have no bottom, and to wander in labyrinthine caverns about the roots of the mountains. The creature had not been very often seen, but Norah well knew what a direful fate had overtaken every soul to whom its shag-maned, lurid-eyed head and rood-length of livid scales had disastrously appeared. One of its least appalling habits, ran report, was to glare fixedly at its victim, until fascinated and distraught he leaped wildly into the jaws gaping for their prey. In the lonesome, murmurous dimness by the shore, Norah did not care to linger over such incidents, and she was turning away quickly, when a shock of fright almost paralysed her. Within a few yards of her feet she saw two reddish amber eyes glowing through the gloom, and from the same place came a sound of something in rustling, flapping motion.

It was, in fact, only a harmless and rather bewildered seal, who, during the past night's turmoil, had somehow got into the lough, and who now, instinctively aware of the rising tide, had set out eager to quit the insipid fresh water for his strong-flavoured Atlantic brine. But Norah naturally jumped to the conclusion that nothing less fearsome than the *Piast* itself was flopping towards her, and she fled away before it in a headlong panic, which culminated a moment afterwards when she ran against some large moving body. This, again, was simply her brother Joe, returned from setting his friends on their way; but Norah, with a wild shriek, gave herself up for lost, and did actually come near putting an end to herself by tumbling in frantic career over one stone, and striking her head violently on another. She had to be carried home insensible, and Christmas Day had come and gone before she found her way back gropingly to conscious-ness.

Meanwhile conjectures, of course, were rife as to the origin of her mishap, and the ante-cedents of the "iligant gold snaky chain" that she was grasping. "Sclutched that tight she had it in her sclenched fist, we were hard set to wrench it out of her hand," Mrs Kenny volubly told her neighbours. The favourite theory held that she "was after pickin' it up on the shore, and would be skytin' home wid it in a hurry, not mindin' where she was goin', and that was the way she got the ugly toss." And when Norah had recovered from the effects of it sufficiently to be asked for her own account of the matter, she could throw but little light thereon. Her accident had left, as so often happens, a strange misty gap in her memory, which it was vain to scan. The space between her first sight of the box and her blinding crash down on the shingle was all a confused blank. However, two results of the affair emerged, and, though their cause remained untraceable, had a distinct influence upon her future. One of them was, that she would on no account permit the snake necklace to be regarded as her property. She persistently asserted that it belonged to Mary and Rose; and when Dr Mason, who had undertaken to dispose of it in Dublin, remitted an incredible number of pounds, she would hear of no arrangement save dividing them between her sister and sister-in-law elect. The other had more important consequences to the whole course of her life. It was an abiding dread of their connecting isthmus, which had become so horrible a place to her that never again would she cross over it, even when promised the protection of the most stalwart escort. Now, as the isthmus is very much the nearest way from the Kennys' farm to any other habitations, this peculiarity of Norah's cut her off greatly from whatever society the neighbourhood afforded, besides gaining her a reputation for "quareness" not likely to increase her popularity. Probably, therefore, it may have been part of the reason why the years as they came and went that way found her rooted fast and growing into a settled old maid.

Those glowering yellow eyes being blurred out of her recollection, the *Piast* did not occur to her as the object of her fear. But some people were not slow to connect it with the uncanny inhabitant of the lough, and in process of time their various imaginations hardened into a circumstantial narrative of an especially terrific appearance of the monster. To this day, indeed, so current is the story, that many a wayfarer along the bleak shingle strip goes the faster for a doubt whether such an awful experience as befell Norah Kenny may not be writhing towards him beneath the sunless waters of Lough Fintragh.

o

THREE PINT MEASURES

THREE PINT MEASURES

THE little stream which flows southward through Ballyhoy must be one of the smallest contributions accepted anywhere by the sea, so insignificant in quantity is the water trickling over the smoothed stone step under the low arch on the shore. Yet the course of its channel can be traced, when the tide is out, in gleaming sky-coloured loops far across the mud-flats. As a rule the tide there *is* out: some of the neighbours indeed, have a theory, no doubt scientifically untenable, that it comes in only about once a week. For this narrow creek, cut off from the Bay by the great grassy sandbank of the North Bull, is steadily silting up, so that its soundings grow shallower every year, and rarer the occasions when we see a plain of sapphire or mother-o'-pearl, threaded with paths of silver rippling, spread all the way between us and the cliffs at purple Howth. It looks as if the Bull would ultimately join the mainland without intermission. Even now, at low water, the passage to

213

and fro can be effected fairly dry-shod by well-chosen routes. These are known to the cattle who graze on the salt herbage among the bent-grown sandhills; and at the fitting time and place, a procession red and white and black may be watched making its way thence in single file towards the strip of common-like pasture beside the sea-road. But the transit, if undertaken by the unwary or ignorant, is beset with serious peril, owing to sundry treacherous mud-holes, which lurk around. Their smothering toils have in time past engulfed much vainly floundering prey, both man and beast, and at the present day several of them are called by the names of their respective victims— Byrne's Hole, Clancy's Hole — obscurely commemorating tragedies not less piteous perhaps than those of the Kelpie's Flow and the Sands of Dee.

I have never heard of any such disaster befalling a class of people who might be supposed peculiarly liable to it, since so much of their time is spent on the dangerous ground. All the shore from Ballyhoy to Portbrendan is haunted by cockle-pickers, who come out from Dublin, where they lodge among the Liberties or other purlieus, climbing down into subterranean cellars, or perhaps mounting wide oaken stairs to spacious upper chambers with the carven panels and mantelpieces and ceilings of the past commenting ironically on the inartistic rags and squalor and famine of to-day. They time their arrival to correspond with low water, so that when you meet a batch of them jogging along the road, you can infer the state of the tide from the contents of the baskets they shoulder, according as these include a heap of grey-fluted shells and a trail of brown seaweed, or nothing except a dull tin measure and a grimy little pipe. Nobody ever sees a cockle-picker apart from his or her basket, yet one of them would be recognised without it, so constant is the type in the species. All are neither young nor old, all are wind and weather beaten, all are short of stature, any original excess in height being compensated for by a more pronounced stoop, and the garments of all reproduce the tints of blackish mud and greenish slime as accurately as if the wearers were animals whose existence depended upon the power of going invisible.

This is not the case, however. Unaggressive and inoffensive in their habits, the cockle-pickers have no especial enemies save the seasons' difference, and the dwellers by the shore regard their proceedings with hardly more suspicion than those of the white sea-gull flocks which sprinkle the neighbouring dark fields, when the lea is broken up and disturbed grubs abound. A favourite fishery is the strand along by the Black Banks, a little to the eastward of the Ballyhoy river; and on most days of the year sombre figures are to be seen there, paddling and poking, barefooted, in the mud, even when the pools have ice at the rim, and the green weed is stiff instead of slimy.

Very differently does the little Black Banks settlement view the coming of some other visitors, who put in an appearance more seldom. But the tinkers are quite used to cool receptions, and if they went only where they were welcome, would find their journeys much restricted. So as this nook offers them a camping ground conveniently accessible from the high road, they occasionally guide their jolting donkey-cart down the shingly track, undeterred by the disapproving eyes that watch them from the adjacent cabin-cluster. One row of these has for some time past been standing roofless, a circumstance which points it out as appropriate quarters for all manner of vagrants, who have forfeited, if indeed they ever possessed, the right to expect the luxury of thatch overhead. And here the tinkers are wont to spend a few weeks every summer, seriously to the discomfort of their temporary neighbours. It must be allowed that they have righteously earned the evil repute which dogs them. Seven ordinarily ingenious magpies would be less grievous to the owners of hen-roosts and other portable property than a single tinker. On many a night odours of savoury cooking, wafted from within the ruined mud walls, have roused rueful suspicions in the proprietor of some "grand young pullet" or "iligant fat duck," which has been mysteriously absent at the last feeding-time; and the stealthiness wherewith a youthful tinker will creep in the small hours of the morning, tin-mug in hand, to milk somebody else's goat tethered behind a rickety-boarded fence, would discredit no Blackfoot on the hunting-trail. Also the tinker men drink and brawl, and the women storm and screech, and the children interminably romp and quarrel, while the whole confraternity use language so wildly bad that it is "fit to rise the hair up off of your head," as scandalised matrons observe standing at their doors, and calling Biddy and Pat and Larry and Rose to "come in out of that and not be listening to such ungovernable talk." And to atone for these causes of offence the tinkers bring no social advantages, if you except now and then the excitement of a stand-up fight between a couple of the men, who have grown pugnacious over their whisky, or the thrilling spectacle of an arrest, which sometimes occurs when the proceedings of the band have come under the consideration of the constabulary in the whitewashed barracks above at Ballyhoy. Dramatic incidents are, be it said, very highly valued hereabouts; but the price of the tinker's performance is more than can be paid without repining.

One day in the course of their last visit, it did seem as if they were going to produce a satisfyingly strong sensation. It came about in this way. Foxy Cullen, their recognised chief, had returned late in the

warm afternoon to the Black Banks from a
tramp round the district with a basket of
tinware. He had not invidiously omitted
to call at the various "publics" which he
passed, and the consequence was that he
now "had drink taken," a state more peril-
ously conducive to rash and reprehensible
acts than downright drunkenness. On the
present occasion, however, nothing more
erratic suggested itself to Foxy than an
idea that he would before he went home
"just step across to the Bull and see what
sort of a place at all it was over there." He
had often wished to do that, and as the tide
had gone black out, leaving no water visibly
intervening, save the river's fine-drawn thread,
the opportunity appeared favourable. So he
set down his basket on the wayside sward,
kept close-shaven by the goats, and he called
to his daughter Peg, whom he saw at hand,
to come along with him. Peg, a queer,
monkey-like little figure in a scarlet print
frock, wore gleeful grins as she obeyed, for
her ragged red-bearded father was to her
the flower and sum of things ; and the pair
walked on over the grass until its daisies
turned into sea-pinks, and until the seaweedy

shingle which succeeded them gave place to a breadth of glistening mud.

By the time they had got so far, Bill Duffy came round the turn of the road, faring homewards with his load of cockles. Bill had had good luck with his fishing that day, and had filled his basket almost before the tide was at its lowest ebb, and it should perhaps be accounted a prolongation of his luckiness that the shimmering tin things in Foxy's basket now beckoned to him from the sunny bank. He concluded that some of the tinkers were about, but he saw nobody near. The tinkers were slight acquaintances of· his, and he had in fact just been trying to negotiate the sale of some of his stock with Mrs Foxy up at the roofless cabin. Unsuccessfully, for she told him with regret that she was "stone broke, and until himself come home, you might all as well be lookin' to find a penny in a cockle-shell as in her ould pocket." To which Bill replied, "Och sure you don't get that on'y in an odd one or so," and departed acquiescent. But this derelict basketful of tinware proved to be a matter less easily dealt with. At first indeed he seemed about to pass it by with

merely a casual glance, which, however, suddenly took on fixity and meaning, as he
stopped short and stood looking earnestly
at the contents. These were mostly tin pint
measures, a dozen of them, maybe, all very
new and clean and shiny.

Now it so happened that at this time Bill
badly wanted such an article. Anybody
might have inferred as much from the dingy,
battered aspect of the little vessel lying atop
of his blackish-grey cockle-heap. In truth,
ever since an accident which it had sustained
a good while ago, it could only by sheer
courtesy be described as a measure at all.
For a dray-horse in Capel Street had set his
shaggy foot upon it, treatment which no bit
of white metal could be expected to endure,
and it had accordingly collapsed into a great
dinge, rendering its capacity henceforth a
question of intricate calculations, far beyond
the tether of Bill or his clients. This unchancy distortion had only the night before
lost him a customer, a housewife who had
" priced " his wares as he passed her half-
door, and showed every symptom of coming
to terms, when an over-officious friend
nudged her elbow, observing " Laws bless

us, woman, look at what he's be way of measurin' them wid. Sure it wouldn't hold a skimpy handful, let alone a pint." Bill protested that it held the biggest pint in the County Dublin, and that he, inconsistently, always allowed the half full of it over and above, to make up for any possible deficiency; nevertheless the prudent matron transferred her patronage to Mary Cassidy, who just then came by, and he was left in the lurch with his damaged mug. But now, when he felt keenly alive both to its shortcomings and to the difficulties of mustering the few pence needed to replace it, here he was all at once confronted with an assortment ready to his hand, nothing apparently interposing to hinder him from acting on the principle that Heaven helps those who help themselves.

Bill Duffy was, as things go, at least indifferent honest; yet his integrity made but a brief stand against the assault thus suddenly sprung upon it. He cast a furtive glance around, and then, with a rapid dive, clutched a measure, and thrust it over his shoulder down deep among his cockles, which rattled clatteringly together to hide the stealth. The next moment he started violently, and felt

certain that he was caught. For at no great
distance there rose up a skirl of shrieking
shriller than had ever issued from sea-fowl's
throat, and looking in the direction of the sound,
he saw a small and gaudy figure running
towards him. It advanced in short rushes, now
and then stopping to dance up and down as if
in an ecstasy of rage or terror, but it screamed
unintermittently, so that Bill could not be sure
whether or no he did hear basser shouts the while
proceeding from a point somewhat farther ·off.
Presently, however, the note of terror grew
predominant enough to change his opinion
about the cause of the outcry, and set him
off trotting to meet it. This red-frocked
screeching child turned out to be Peg Cullen,
and the burden of her lamentations was something unintelligible concerning " Daddy," whose
bawls in the background here became, fortunately for him, so distinct as to furnish an
explanatory note. Foxy had evidently blun-
dered into a mud-hole, which was now, in
conformity with its agreeable custom, taking
prompt steps to secure and secrete him. Bill
rapidly grasped the situation, and unhitching
his heavy basket he detached its long strap,
and sped to the rescue, which, as Foxy was not

yet very deeply engaged, he found himself able to effect. A few frantic plunges and desperate hauls set Foxy on firm ground, exceedingly miry and alarmed, and quite sober ; Peg left off screaming and dancing, and they all returned to the road, stepping gingerly while they were on the mud, but stamping boldly once they felt the dry sod under their feet.

When they came where the tinker's basket was, Foxy fell to emptying his black-oozing brogues, whilst Bill, case-hardened by much wading, began to splice his strap, which had nearly marred all with symptoms of fracture during the last critical tug. He had for the time being forgotten all about the pint measure. By-and-by, however, Foxy, flinging away the grass-wisp he had used to wipe off the mud, and shuffling uncomfortably in his soaked boots, said with a dissatisfied grunt, " Augh, bad luck to it for a deceptionable ould brash. I may go now and get another sup of somethin' or else it 's destroyed I 'll be wid the could creeps in me bones agin mornin' ; wud you take a glass, man ? "

" Sure, no," said Bill ; " I 'm shankin' into town meself as soon as I can get th' ould strap mended."

"That's not much of a concern you've got there," said Foxy, pointing to Bill's old mug as it lay dinted side uppermost on his cockles; "past mendin' it is, I should say. Look-a, here's a somethin' better quality you'd be welcome to." He held out one of his measures to Bill, who shrank back as if its glittering surface had been incandescent with white-heat. The consciousness of what was hidden in the depths of his basket seemed to scorch his face and dazzle his eyes.

"Och, not at all, thank 'ee," he said; "sure this I have usin' does grand; it's the handiest one I ever owned. And I have a couple or so of spare ones lyin' about at home if I would be wantin' them. Och, not at all."

"It's a quare fancy you'd be havin', then, to go about wid the likes of that," said Foxy. "Musha, man, how ready you are to make a lie and tell it. Sure it's no compliment to be takin' such a trifle off me, when I've got a basket full of them, and morebetoken I couldn't say how many quarts of the bastely black mud I mightn't be after swallyin' down agin now if·it wasn't only for you lendin' me a hand out— bejabers it was the sizeablest cockle you ever landed. Bad cess to the could wather, it's at

P

the bottom of every manner of mischief. I'm steppin' along for a drop of spirits, and I'll lave the bit of a mug wid you, whether or no." He thrust it into Bill's basket and went off, followed jealously by Peg.

For a moment Bill stood staring blankly after them, but then an idea suggested itself, and hoisting his basket on his arm he started in the opposite direction.

At his goal, which was the tinker's cabin, he found Mrs Foxy stooping over her smoky driftwood fire, in a "quare ugly temper," as her family could have told him. "Whethen now and is it yourself botherin' back agin?" she said upon seeing him; "didn't I tell you a while ago as plain as I could spake that we weren't wantin' cockles to-day?"

"Ah whisht, honey, and don't be strikin' up ahead of the fiddler," said Bill suavely. "Amn't I just after meetin' himself out there, and he biddin' me be bringin' you up three pints for your suppers?"

Mrs Foxy's countenance cleared up. "Well, tubbe sure," she said; "it's not often the man has the wit or the money left to do anythin' so raisonable wid this hour of the evenin'. But they'll come in oncommon handy, for it's cleared out we are to-night intirely. What all I have for the supper wouldn't pacify a scutty wren."

The whole Cullen family looked on with a sense of brightened prospects while Bill dropped the cockles resonantly into a tin can. It is part of Fate's irony towards the tinkers that, however plentiful may be the lack of viands in their larder, they are always abundantly provided with cooking utensils. He meted out his three pints with a reckless liberality which convinced Mrs Foxy that her husband must have ordered, and paid for, a couple of quarts at least. And when he took his departure, he successfully accomplished the stratagem, which had been the main object of his visit, by laying down, unperceived, Foxy's glowing gift upon a nettle-girt stone just inside the threshold. This done, he went on his way greatly relieved and self-conciliated.

But he had not trudged many paces before scurrying feet pursued and overtook him. Somebody had espied the purposely forgotten measure, and had remarked: "Och, he's after lavin' his mug behind him"; upon which somebody else rejoined: "'Deed, then, we've slathers of them litterin' about widout it, so there's no good keepin' it on the man. Skyte after him wid it, Lizzie." And Lizzie skyted, sped by a desire to be but briefly absent from the scene of preparations for supper, so that she tossed the mug into Bill's basket with scant ceremony, and was off again ere he well knew what had befallen. When it grew clear, a leaden conviction dumped down on him that he might give up setting his wits against Destiny. "Sure it was to be," he said to himself drearily, as he resumed his plodding, bent dejectedly under a heavier weight than his moist basket. He resorted rather frequently to this obvious truth, whence•we may infer that his stock of consolatory reflections was not extensive.

When he came once more where the road crossed the river, he, according to custom in warm weather, climbed down the grassy bank for a drink. On this occasion, however, his first act was to take all his three pint measures out of the basket and set them in a row— the one he had been given, and the one he had stolen, and the battered old one that had, in a manner, caused the whole difficulty. Bill eyed them gloomily as they glinted in the long rays. "Troth, it's themselves are the iligant lookin' collection," he said to himself with some resentment, "and a grand ould slieveen's trick it was to be thievin' a poor man's bit of property, and he all the time widin two twos of dhrowndin' dead, scarce a stone's - throw away. Ay, bedad, it was so. But, musha, it was to be." As he mused mutteringly, he picked up a mug at random and dipped it carelessly in the stream, but something surprising followed. For the water it scooped up straightway plashed out of it again, as if poured through a funnel. Of course, Bill investigated the reason of this, and the result was a discovery which lit up his face with a broad grin. Through some detect in the soldering, the bottom of the vessel had almost detached itself from the rim, and flapped out like a swing door at the slightest touch. It could, clearly, hold nothing ; and it was the stolen mug—he re-cognised it by the handle.

"Bless me ould bones, look at that now," Bill said gleefully, "you might all as well be axin' wather to stop aisy in the holes of me ould basket here. Sure it wouldn't hould e'er a hap'orth of anythin' wet or dhry "—he dropped a handful of cockles into it, and triumphantly watched them slip through and fall with tiny thuds on the grass. "Ay, begorra, it'd ha' never been a thraneen of use to man or mortal; ne'er a brass bawbee was it worth all the time, glory be to God."

He gloated over its dilapidations for a while longer, and at last poked it in behind a stone under the arch, where, for aught I know, it may remain to the present day. Then he gathered up the rest of his effects, and finally resumed his interrupted journey Dublin-wards, facing a sky where the sunset grew as golden as the light in a crocus-cup. But he no longer muttered: "It was to be." The burden of his meditations was: "Bedad now, it's a good job I happened to be widin hearin' of their roars, or else they might be lettin' them yet. And belike I wouldn't ha' been, if it wasn't only be raison of me stoppin' to—to—to look at them pint mugs."

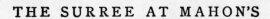

THE SURREE AT MAHON'S

THE SURREE AT MAHON'S

FEW people, I think, can ever have been impressed by the liveliness of little Killymeen, set in its nook among the lonesome mountain and moorland, its one humble street forming the nucleus of a sparse cabin-sprinkling, which strews white flecks on the far sweeping green folds hardly plentier than hailstones on a grass plot half a sunny hour after a July thunderstorm. Yet to Bridget Doran, the girl who had lately taken service with the Caseys up at the Quarry Farm, it seemed a centre of fashion and gaiety, being, indeed, the most considerable place she had seen in all her seventeen years. For they had been spent up at Loughdrumesk, a hamlet fully ten miles deeper among the wildest townlands, with only a rough cart-track threading a black bog, and climbing endless shaggy slopes, and dropping over a purple mountain shoulder to connect it with Killymeen. She had left behind there, three months ago, her feeble old grandfather and alert old grandmother, in a tiny, high-perched cabin, which felt a world too wide for its other indwellers when this third of their lives had gone. And since then there had been much travelling of thoughts to and fro between it and the Casey's prim whitewashed farmhouse at the foot of Slieve Glasarna. At first Bridget's had made the journey as constantly as her grandmother's, but she was young and busy and in a new place, and as the weeks went on she became more engrossed with what lay immediately before her.

The Surree at Mahon's, fixed for a day in Christmas week, was the most exciting of the fresh prospects that unfolded themselves, and was looked forward to with much pleased interest by Killymeen at large. There had •been no Surrees in the neighbourhood during a long spell of bad times, but this year matters were looking brighter, and old Barney Mahon, who had a thrifty turn and a commodious kitchen, was encouraged to make a venture which promised fair profits at a small risk. For a Surree, which has with quaint effect borrowed its name from polite French, is a sort of subscription dance, little more elaborate in its

arrangements than are the kaleys, or con-
versazioni, that beguile so many wintry
hours in Donegal homes, when all the dark
out-of-doors hurtles and splashes with wind
and rain, and the neighbours drift into their
places round some appointed hearth as
promiscuously as a wreath of dry leaves
swept rustling together by an aerial eddy.
At a Surree each couple pay a shilling, but
no refreshment is expected save frugally-
dispensed tea; and the fiddler is content to
scrape for a modest fee and his chances of
small coins from the dancers. Dark Hugh
M'Evoy, being Barney's cousin, was willing
to supply the music for this occasion on
specially easy terms; and, in short, circumstances conspired to make it seem desirable
that Barney should meet the often-expressed
wish of his younger friends by announcing
the first Surree of the season.

It would be Bridget's first taste of any
formal dissipation, and Rose Casey, her
master's niece, and Kate Duffy, his plough-
man's daughter, who lived in the yard, set
her expectation on tiptoe extremely by their
accounts of like entertainments. Kate and
she were to go together, as it is the custom

to attend Surrees in couples. These often are formed of a colleen with the boy who is "spakin'" to her, but often also a brother and sister make a pair, or any other two friends. Rose Casey was to marry Peter O'Donoghue at Shrovetide, so she would, of course, go with him—a fact of which she made a little parade to Bridget, who felt, however, perfectly content with Kate's escort: a sweetheart of her own would have seemed, indeed, an alarming possession. Her mistress had advanced her a shilling out of her quarter's wages—a whole pound — and she had expended the sixpence left after securing her admission to the Surree upon a splendid red glass brooch, which made her think her equipment very complete.

But just when everything seemed gliding most smoothly towards the delightful goal, an obstacle suddenly cropped up and threatened to overthrow all her plans with one disastrous jolt. On a certain frost-spangled morning the postman brought to Bridget a letter, whose contents agreed with her wishes as ill as a dash of vinegar would have done with the thick cream which she was churning when the mail arrived. Her grandmother wrote to say that "she thought bad of Biddy to be trampin' the long way her lone from Killymeen to their place, and that old Bill Molloy was slippin' over wid his pony and a gatherin' of eggs to the Magamore on next Thursday morning, and 'd give her a lift if she 'd start along wid him when he would be goin' back. So Biddy had a right to ax lave of her mistress, and come home wid ould Bill, who 'd turn a bit out of his way to pick her up? and real glad they 'd be to set eyes on her again." For Mrs Casey had promised Biddy her choice of three days in Christmas week to spend at home, dairy work being slack. Bridget had looked forward to the holiday with a glow of pleasure, and meant to take it on the Friday, which would be Christmas Eve, and the day after the Surree. But her grandmother's injunction was not compatible with this arrangement.

"Sure I 'd miss all the fun and everythin' if I took off and went wid ould Bill—I wish he and his baste of an ugly skewbald 'd keep themselves out of botherin' where they arn't wanted," she said, half-crying, to her friends Rose and Kate, as she showed them the letter in the kitchen.

"Musha, good gracious," said Rose, "you wouldn't ever think of goin'? Just bid the ould man step along wid himself, and say you'll come on Friday."

"But me grandmother'd be rale vexed if I done that, and he after goin' out of his road to call for me," said Bridget doubtfully.

"Well, then," said Kate, "you might write and tell her not to send him. This is only Tuesday; there's plenty of time yet, and I've a stamp in me box this long while you're welcome to."

"Ay, to be sure," said Rose, "and say me aunt can't spare you convanient afore Friday."

"But," said Bridget, looking disconcerted, "I'm after sendin' her word be Judy Flynn that I'd got lave to come any day at all this week."

"Oh, botheration to it," said Rose. "Then say you're too bad with a cowld, and couldn't be thravellin' that far. Bedad, I heard you coughin' this mornin' fit to fall in pieces like the head of the witherdy geranium there. Morebetoken, the red one in the windy corner's dhroppin' itself into the pan of buttermilk where you've set it; you'd better be movin' it out of that."

"I have a heavy cowld on me sure enough," said Bridget, coughing to convince herself, but her disconcerted expression remained, and she fidgetted about uneasily. "For the matter of writin'," she said, "you see the time I was gettin' me schoolin' I did be mostly mindin' the sheep, and I can make some sort of an offer at the readin' if it's wrote pretty big, but writin' oneself is quare nigglety work."

"Mercy on us, girl alive, if that's all that ails you, I'll write a letter for you meself in a minyit and a half," said Rose with alacrity. "Bedad will I. Sure I've wrote to Peter times and again when he was stoppin' away at Manchester. So don't bother your head about it; lave the regulation of it to me. I've plenty of paper meself, and Kate'll give me her stamp."

Bridget agreed to this plan, though not without some qualms of conscience, which made her refrain guiltily from inquiring about the details of its execution, thereby giving Rose a free hand, of which she availed herself without much scruple. She had an imaginative turn of mind, and a taste for fiction, so her story grew under her scratching pen until in the end she produced a letter purporting to come not from Bridget, but from herself, and describing Bridget's indisposition as not a simple cold, but an attack of "plussery-newmoney." This formidable complaint would hinder her from returning with Bill Molloy. "But she'll come," wrote Rose, "as soon as ever she's able. And that won't be before Friday anyway, if she overs it at all." The last clause struck her as giving an effective completeness to the composition, and she read it over with a complacency which did not take into account how it might be spelled out in the bleak little hill-side cabin off away at Loughdrumesk.

The evening of the Surree arrived in due course, and with it a flutter of snow, swirling on rough and unruly blasts. Silver-white threads and stitches had begun to embroider the purple folds of Slieve Glasarna before the mists descended muffling and blurring; and the paths crunched crisply under brogues, and made cold clutches at bare feet by the time that the neighbours were approaching Barney Mahon's door. They remarked to one another that it was hardy weather, and added that they were apt to have it "sevare,"

which is some degree worse than hardy.
Few people, however, had been daunted into
staying at home, and there was much shaking
of powder flakes out of shawl-folds and off
rough coat-sleeves at the entrance to Barney's
lustily flickering room.

When Rose and Kate and Bridget got
there, which they did as soon as ever they
could finish "readying up" after tea, most
of the company had assembled, and dancing
was about to begin. Rose's temper was
somewhat ruffled because Peter O'Donoghue
had not kept his promise of coming to
escort her. But his sisters now hastened to
explain how he had been delayed by the
sudden illness of their calf. "Howane'er the
baste was comin' round finely when they
left," they reported, and Peter would be
after them in no time. So his *fiancée* was
appeased, and contented herself provision-
ally with Larry Sullivan for a partner. "Faix,
now, it's on'y an odd turn the rest of us
boys gets wid you these times," he said to
her gallantly as the fiddler struck up. "Ne'er
a chance we have at all, unless when the
luck keeps him that's luckier away."

Do not suppose that the Surree danced jigs.

Q

Later on in the evening a couple might stand up and perform one while the others were recovering their breath; but at the outset it was a vigorous round dance that began to gyrate with a step which, though perhaps not recognised in any academy, kept time to Hugh's music with much accuracy, and made light of the difficulties opposed by an uneven mud floor. The crockery on the dresser jingled merrily to the rhythmical beat of their feet; and each pair of bobbing heads that passed in front of it, might be seen to make an abrupt dip down and up again. This was caused by an unusually deep hollow which occurred in that part of the floor, and Barney Mahon, looking on with the elders from their circle round the hearth, observed it and said—" Begob, I must see to having that houle filled up before next time, or else somebody'll be trippin' up in it, and gettin' a quare toss."

The other spectators sat well content with their share of the entertainment. Pungently-puffing cutty pipes solaced the men, and the women kept their knitting needles twinkling; in fact, they would almost as soon have left off breathing by way of rest and relaxation.

For further amusement they had the affairs of the countryside to discuss, enlivened by an occasional anecdote or riddle. Dan Goligher had just propounded one of the latter which successfully puzzled everybody who had not heard it before—

A brown lough
Wid a white strand,
Sorra the ship could sail around it,
But I can hould it in my hand;

and he was triumphantly explaining, "Sure a cup of tea," when two people came bolting in at the door, which they forthwith began to secure behind them, as if they were shutting out some deadly peril. They said nothing, but their speechless hurry was more suggestive than words.

"Whethen now, Peter O'Donoghue and Ned Kinsella, what's took you at all to be flouncin' in on the people that a-way?" said Barney Mahon, somewhat affronted at their unceremonious entrance and dealings with his fastenings and furniture. "That's a great ould slammin' of the door you have—and what for would you be jammin' the bench again it, unless you're intendin' the next body that comes thro' it to be breakin' his shins?"

"Troth, I on'y hope it may—and its neck too, between us and harm—if it's offering to come in on us—I do so," said Peter O'Donoghue, panting. He left his comrade to finish barricading the door, and pushed himself farther into the room, until several groups interposed between him and the dangerous point. "After us it may be this minyit of time," he said. "Och, but that was the quare fright I got; the saints look down upon us this night!"

"It's herself below at th' ould gate there," said Ned Kinsella, who was calmer than Peter, though evidently much alarmed. "And more-be-token it's not inside she is this night, but sittin' crouched up on the bank be the path, and the grab she made at Peter going by; 'deed, I thought he'd never get his coat-tail wrenched out of her ould hand."

"It might as well ha' been caught in a rat-trap the way she held on," said Peter. "I give you me word me hair's standin' on end yet, fit to rise me hat off the roof of me head. What wid that and the onnathural screeches she let, I won'er you didn't hear them here. And it's my belief she set off leggin' after us—goodness preserve us—on'y

I was afraid of me life to look round and see."

These tidings spread general consternation among the company, as under the circumstances they well might do. For only a few hundred yards down the loaning lay an ancient burying-ground, with its ruined chapel and weed-entangled tombstones, a place whose ghostly reputation had long been established at Killymeen. In particular the wraith of a little old woman was often to be seen of an evening peering out through the rusty gate-bars, and sometimes stretching forth a fearsome hand to pluck at the unwary passer-by. But her appearance out on the roadside was a new development, and one which made Peter and Ned's report unpleasant hearing for people who would presently be obliged to take that route home. The dance came to a standstill, and in its stead a series of dismal ghost-stories began to circle round the room. Perhaps the most gruesome of them was Nick Carolan's. He related how he had once lived in a place where there was in the middle of the yard a deep well, out of which on certain moonlit nights a dark figure would emerge and go gliding round and round it, making a wider and wider circuit, until she reached the house, at whose door she rapped loudly as she passed by. And whenever that happened there would be a death in the family before the twelvemonth was out as sure as fate. A general shudder followed this *dénouement*, and old Mrs Linders made a particular application of it by remarking gloomily that it was a poor case to have the likes of such crathurs about; but Mrs Coleman, a comely matron, who continued to sit by the fire unperturbed, said placidly in a pause, "Sorra a bit of harm there's in it this night I'm a-thinkin'. If the lads seen anythin', it's apt to ha' just been some poor body after missin' her way in the snow."

"Troth and bedad, then it was the quare body altogether," Peter asseverated, "and the hair of me head, as I was tellin' you, bristlin' straight wid the dhread of her the first minyit I come nigh the place."

"Ah, sure, some people's as ready at that as a dog at cockin' his ears," said Joey Nolan. "Maybe we'd a right to go look is there e'er a one in it. Some crathur might be strayin' about perishin', and it snowin' again as thick as sheep's wool."

"Begor you won't persuade me to go foolin' along wid you," said Peter; "I couldn't be gettin' my heels out of it fast enough. May the saints have me sowl, but I thought I'd lose me life afore ever I landed inside—and here I'll stop. Nobody need be axin' me, for divil a fut I'll stir."

"Good people are scarce," Joe observed sarcastically; but Peter went on in a half-complacent tone, "One while it'll be afore I'm the better of that frightenin' I got. Every mortal bit of me's in a thrimble wid it yet."

"Musha, then, you gaby, can't you whisht about it, instead of to be tellin' everybody the sort of ould polthroon you are?" Rose Casey whispered to him fiercely, ready to cry with mortification as she saw significant smiles passing round at the expense of her happily unconscious betrothed.

As she spoke, the door resounded with a heavy thump, which made those who were standing next it hop back with a scarcely dignified haste. Some of them tried to carry it off by pretending that they were merely getting out of one another's way, while some shrieked unfeignedly, and above all ejaculations rose Peter O'Donoghue's voice, shrill with undissembled terror, saying: "Oh to goodness, don't open it for your lives. Run that other form again it, you that are widin raich. Mercy be among us, she's apt to have us all destroyed."

"Arrah, now, will you be lettin' us in out of that, you jackasses, you?" shouted a voice reassuringly familiar and irate. It was young Larry Sullivan, who had slipped out through the back door a few minutes before, and whose impatience at being kept waiting had nothing supernatural about it. Despite Peter's remonstrances, the door was thrown open, and disclosed Larry, standing tall against a background of glimmering white, in a gloom which, when you looked into it anywhere steadily, grew full of wandering flakes like scattered bread-crumbs. Beside him appeared a smaller figure, whom he pulled indoors along with him before anybody well had time for terrific surmises, and whom the firelight showed to be a little old woman, wrapped up in a powdered brown shawl. She was breathless and bewildered and forlorn-looking, as she peered round from face to face, all strange, all comfortless—but no!

for the moment Bridget Doran set eyes on her she sprang at her and caught her in a great hug—

"Why, granny darlint, and is it yourself?" she said. "And how at all did you come this night in the snow? It's kilt you are entirely. You can't ever ha' come wid ould Bill Molloy?"

"Ah, honey, I thramped it," said old Mrs Doran. "Sure I couldn't rest aisy, thinkin' me little Biddy was took that bad away all her lone among the strange people. But finely you're looking, glory be to goodness. 'Deed now me heart's been fit to break frettin' ever since I got the letter this mornin', sayin' that belike you wouldn't get over it."

"An' I to be dancin' round like a zany bewitched, and you all the while streelin' through the snow," said Bridget, with acute remorse. "It's sorry I am that I let anybody send you such owld lies. But"— looking indignantly at Rose—"I only said to say that I had a cowld."

"And I lost me way in the dark," went on Mrs Doran plaintively, "and what at all I'd ha' done I dunno, on'y for the dacint boy coming by, for nought else the other two'd do but let yells at me, and run away like scared turkeys."

"Creepin' along under the high bank she was, the crathur, when I met her," Larry meanwhile was telling the others, "and scarce able to contind wid the blasts of the win'. And sez she to me, 'For the love of God, just stop to tell me am I anywhere near the Casey's house?' And sez I to her, 'Is it the Quarry Farm you're wantin'?' And sez she to me, 'Ay, it's where my poor Katey's little daughter Bridget Doran's in service, and dyin' wid some manner of outlandish sickness: It's to her, I'm goin',' sez she. So sez I to her, if it was Bridget Doran she was wantin', I'd seen the girl three minyits ago, and ne'er a sign of dyin' on her whatsome'er, and I just brought her along here. It's perished and stupid the crathur is wid the cowld. You'd a right to get her a cup of hot tay, and a warm at the fire," concluded Larry, thereupon bestirring himself to superintend the carrying out of this prescription. And a little later he prompted his mother to offer Mrs Doran a night's lodging at their house close by, thus entailing upon themselves more hospitality than they had foreseen.

For of the Surree at Mahon's all's well
that ends well could not quite be said, as
some of the guests were disposed to say
prematurely when the assembly was breaking
up. To begin with, old Mrs Doran had
caught a very bad chill during her snowy
wanderings, and now had a severe illness
which endangered her life, and obliged
Bridget to pay many an anxious and
conscience-stricken hour as a fee for her
deceptive letter, while a difference which she
had next morning with Rose Casey about
the unauthorised mendacity of its contents
led to a permanent cooling down of their
friendship. Moreover, Rose, on the very
same day, spoke in such scathing terms to
Peter O'Donoghue with reference to his
panic on the night before, that even his
impenetrable self-satisfaction was touched,
and a violent falling out ensued. The consequence was that no wedding took place at
Shrovetide; and the last time I had news
from Killymeen "there was no talk of it
at all, at all," so the breach may be considered final. In fact, it is commonly supposed
that he has some notion of transferring his
attentions to Bridget Doran. But I happen

to know that the only one among the boys she thinks anything of is Larry Sullivan, whom she always remembers gratefully as the rescuer of her grandmother. Whereas, if Larry fancies anyone, it is Kate Duffy.

Whence it appears that some rather complicated cross currents in the stream of life flowing through Killymeen have started from this Surree at Mahon's.

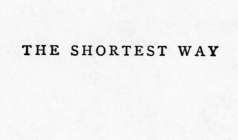

THE SHORTEST WAY

THE SHORTEST WAY

DISTRICT-INSPECTOR ROCHFORT had risen very early on that wet August morning, to go trout-fishing along the Feltragh River. He hoped to get a couple of hours at it before breakfast; so he was not best pleased when Hugh Christie accosted him as he crossed the Ivy Bridge. Hugh was looking over the wreathed parapet up the river, and did not take his eyes off it; only put out a hand as Mr Rochfort passed, and stopped him with a touch on the arm. Undoubtedly Hugh had queer ways. His neighbours pronounced him to be "not all there," which seemed an inappropriate description of his peculiarities, as rather there was more of him than of other people. But the more was something uncanny. He now said, still watching the water: "I was thinkin' the Sargint might come by; howsome'er, sir, you'll do as well."

"That I won't, my man," said Mr Rochfort, "unless it can be done uncommonly smart, for I've no time to waste."

"It's as short as it's long," said Hugh. "But

you needn't mind about *thim*"—he pointed to the young man's rod and creel—"there'll be none of that work till it's gone down, and risin' it'll be yet awhile."

Mr Rochfort looked where Hugh was looking, and had reluctantly to admit the truth of this. The river ran far below them, down in a narrow steep-walled little glen, one of the many cracks that fissure Lisvaughan's wind-swept, limestone plain. Almost each of these ravines has a stream in it, with a remnant of trees huddled together for shelter from the storms, whose stress they dare not meet in the open, and with ferns venturing out of the rock-clefts to droop ample fronds over the boulders on the margin. It is thus with Feltragh River, which rises in the moorland towards Shrole, and here, at the Ivy Bridge, comes round a sharp turn down a very stony stair. On the other side of the arch it broadens slightly, and a somewhat longer reach of it is in view; but Hugh Christie was staring up-stream, where the water rushed into sight abruptly within a pebble's cast of his station. Swirling and tumbling it came, thrusting thick glassy strands between the boulders, or seething

over the tallest of them in creamy fleeces. A
roar ascended from those rapids hollowly and
fitfully, so that the District-Inspector looked
up and down the road occasionally, thinking
a heavy cart must be lumbering along.

"There's a strong current in it now," said
Hugh. "Man nor mortal couldn't stand agin
it. 'Twould lift a dead cow, let alone—anything else."

"You've chosen a good place for a drench-
ing," said the District-Inspector, for the wind
was driving its cold spray into their faces;
"but I don't see what else is to be got by
staying in it." And he was moving on, when
Hugh said—

"Just wait a bit, till I tell you."

Hugh's clothes had a sodden appearance,
as if they had given up trying to get any
wetter, and his brown beard was all in a
silvery mist of tiny drops; therefore he
was not sensitive about the dampness of the
weather. But what he said, though the
District-Inspector did wait, was nothing more
to the purpose than: "Last night was powerful dark; but it didn't settle to rain till goin'
on for one o'clock—not to spake of, any
way."

R

"Well, it's making up for lost time now, at all events," said the District-Inspector, and had to be stopped again.

"See here, Mr Rochfort, you're newish to the place; but ax anybody—ax his Riverence, or Mr Lennon at the public, or Sargint Moore—and every one of them'll say I was niver known to raise a hand to do murdher on man or woman — or I might say child," Hugh added after a pause, as if he felt that he was making large demands upon credulity.

"If I were you, Christie, I'd go home, out of the rain," replied the District-Inspector.

"Och, no matther for that. I was goin' to ax you, sir, did you remember the McAuliffes —the widdy and her daughter: that was all of them was in it, ever since you come to Lisvaughan."

"Who lived at Brierly's cottages over yonder?" the District-Inspector said, pointing towards the smooth-faced crag whose jut prevented them from seeing any farther up the Feltragh River. "I believe I do remember the old woman creeping to Mass—a little lame body; didn't she die the other day?"

"Ay did she, last Friday week in Shrole Union; for the daughter that kep' her out of

it went wid the fever in the spring, and her
son Dan that ped their rint in 'Sthralia, was
niver sendin' her a word iver since. So she
made up her mind he was dead too, and she
didn't care what become of her after that; and
she broke her heart fretting in the Infirm'ry.
But last night Dan landed home lookin' for
her, as plased as anythin'."

"The unlucky devil," said the District-
Inspector.

"You may say that," said Hugh; "but
there's unluckier. Sure it was meself met
him a trifle down the road, and on'y for that,
'twould ha' been nobody's doin', and done all
the same. And if it hadn't been that out-
rageous dark, I'd never ha' seen a sight of
him. But sure up agin ourselves we foosthered
on the path, and I wasn't long then doubtin'
who had the discourse out of him about the
Divil and such. So: 'Is it after desthroyin'
you, I am, Dan?' sez I. And sez he, 'To
your sowl, if it's yourself, Hughey Christie,'
he sez, for he and I did be as thick as thieves
in the ould times. And 'Come a step along
wid me,' sez he, 'for I can't be delayin'.'
'Sure where's the hurry at all?' sez I, mis-
doubtin' what might be in his mind, if he

knew no betther or worser. 'Why, man,' sez
he, 'isn't it goin' on for ten year since I was
at home? And like a living dhrame to me
now I'm thinkin' I'm that near her agin.' So
sez I to myself, 'The Divil's in it'; and sez
I to himself, 'Take care it isn't too soon you'll
be gettin' there, since you couldn't conthrive
it any sooner.' Sure now, you'd ha' supposed
he'd ha' had the wit to git a fright at that.
But all he said was, 'Ah,—the sisther, poor
Lizzie, the crathur; 'deed, then, that was the
great pity entirely, and a cruel loss to her
for sartin. But sure that's the raisin of me
comin' home at all, thinkin' me mother'd be
left too lonesome altogether. And what wid
th' ould stame-boat bustin' up in her ingines,'
sez he, 'and meself takin' bad where they
stopped for repeers, I've been twyste the time
I'd a right to on the way. She'll be in dhread
there's somethin' happint me. Howane'er, sorra
a much fear of that is there now, Hughey man,
and me, so to spake, at the door goin' in to
her, thanks be to goodness,' sez he.

"And niver a word out of me head to that.
But I declare to you, sir, you might ha'
thought the river itself, that's a dumb crathur,
was thryin' its best to tell him, accordin' to

the quare mutterin' like it kep' on wid down
below. For stumpin' up the Quarry Lane he
was, that's the nearest road to his house; 'twas
just turnin' into it I met him. Nor aisy it
wouldn't ha' been any ways to git a word
into the talk he had, and it mostly all about
what he'd saved in 'Sthralia, and the fine
counthry it was, and the grand thing to ha'
got away out of it. 'But,' sez he, 'maybe I'd
ha' sted in it a while longer, if I hadn't been
afeard me ould woman here'd get mopin' and
frettin' left all to herself, which I couldn't abide
the thoughts of. For right well I was doin' out
there,' sez he, 'and in another couple of years
I'd ha' had a goodish bit more to be bringin'
home wid me.' And, bedad, you could see
the truth of that, because every glimmer of
light in the black of the night was shinin' on
the len'ths of the gould watch-chain he had
wearin' on his weskit. 'Howiver,' he sez,
'I've plinty to be keepin' her iligant, and
what great matther about anythin' more,
when herself's the on'y mortal crathur I
have belongin' to me in the width of the
world? Sure, if I hadn't her to be spendin'
it on,' sez he, 'I'd as lief be slingin' ivery
blamed ould pinny I own over the bank there

into the rowlin' river, and meself after it —
faix would I, the Lord knows.'

"Well now, sir, after his sayin' that, wouldn't
tellin' him ha' been as good as biddin' him
go dhrownd himself? I put it to you:
wouldn't it now?"

"It's hard to say," said the District-Inspector: "but what *did* you do?"

"Stumpin' along wid him I was, lettin' on
I was listenin' to him, and all the while I was
makin' no more sinse of it than if he'd been a
bullock I had dhrivin' to market, that would be
lettin' a roar now and agin, at the mischief
knows what. For thinkin' to meself I was that
unless I quitted foolin' him, he'd be very
prisintly walkin' up to his door, and one of
the Duggans, that he niver set eyes on in his
life, shoutin' to know who he was, and what
he wanted, and tellin' him the Union was
after buryin' his mother on him. So at last
I'd twisted up me mind wid the notion I'd
spake out the next time he said anythin', and
if I did, that minyit he hit me a clout on the
back, and, ' Och, Hughey, you bosthoon,' sez
he, ' herself 'll be sittin' this instiant of time
be the fire in there, and niver thinkin' I'm
comin' along a few perch down the ould road.'

"And sez I, 'Tubbe sure, Dan, she's thinkin'
no such thing at all'; and, for that matther,
what truer could I ha' said? And as sure as
I'm alive, I'd ha' gone on wid it, I would so,
on'y 'twas just then we come round the turn
opposite them Brierly Cottages. You know,
sir, where they're cocked up, across the river,
fornint Fitzsimmons' lime-kiln, wid ne'er a
handy way of gittin' at them except be the
bridge; the next one above this it is—a
wooden fut-bridge wid a hand-rail. But not a
sight of it could we see in the dark, or anythin'
else, on'y the light burnin' in the Duggans'
windy, the way it used to be afore they come
there.

"And when Dan seen that, he let a sort of
yell, and sez he, 'There it is—there's her ould
bit of a lamp lightin' the same as it was ever,
and meself beholdin' it agin—*glory be to God.*'
The Divil's in it," Hugh said, with a fierce
clutch at the dripping ivy-sprays. "If the
crathur hadn't been so ready to be gloryin'
God, I'd ha' found it in me heart to ha' tould
him the whole thing straight out—goodness
help him!—but instead of that, I thought to
be comin' at it gradial. So I sez to him,
lettin' on I wasn't mindin' what he'd said,

'Is it a star you're lookin' at?' And sez he to me, 'Musha, not at all, man; it's somethin' a dale nearer than a one of thim.' And, 'There's things farther off than stars,' sez I; and, 'Belike there is,' sez he, 'but I'm not apt to be throublin' me head about them when me ould woman's waitin' for me unbeknownst just across the sthrame. So I'll be sayin' good-night to you kindly, Hughey, and skytin' over. Where at all's the bridge? I can't make out a stim before me. Ah, here it is!' sez he, 'right enough in its own place.'

"And it's the truth I'm tellin' you, Mr Rochfort, the truth I'm tellin' you: not till the man was grabbin' the rail wid one hand and mine wid the other, biddin' me good-night, did the recollection come into me mind of anythin' amiss. And then I dunno rightly how it was, but the same time I got considherin' the way 'twould be, supposin' I held me tongue for that minyit. For if I didn't tell him the one thing, nobody'd ever tell him the other, and 'twould save throuble in a manner. Och, I dunno what come over me, but in the end all I sez to him was, 'You'll have to be walkin' cautious, Dan,'—God forgive me, but for sure He won't: that was every word I said."

"But why should you have said more?" asked the District-Inspector. "The bridge is safe enough. Wasn't the man sober?"

"Safe enough, begorra!" said Hugh. "If there warn't six fut smashed slap out of the middle of it wid the big ash-tree buttin' its head through it, that was blown off the top of the bank in the storm the night before last. Six fut clever and clane, and maybe six times six fut under it to drop down on the river and the rocks." ·

"And you sent him over that in the dark?" said the District-Inspector. "What on earth possessed you?" This question, however, was merely a phrase, for he seemed to know the reason very well. "Was he killed?" he demanded, with the inquest in his mind. "Where's the body lying?"

"It's that I'm watchin' for," said Hugh, his eyes still following the rough white race below, "ever since I had light to see. He might be comin' by any minyit now. But until the river riz wid the rain a couple of hours back, I doubt was there water enough to bring him; there was no very great dale runnin' in it before then. So I wouldn't think he could ha' slipped past, and I not to notice."

"Do you mean to say," said the District-Inspector, "that you went off and left the unfortunate man there, without so much as ascertaining whether he was dead or alive?"

"Alive is it?" said Hugh. "Sure the wooden bridge is a good bit higher than this one; but if I tuk a standin' lep off of the ledge here, it's breakin' me neck I'd be afore I knew where I was. And the jagged lumps of big stones is terrible; he might be wedged in between two of them. Och, no! for all the life's left in him, poor Dan'll ha' had a paicibler night of it up there than meself had here, considherin' quare things in the dark this long while. Ay will he, for the sort of moanin' and screeches there was in it now and again was nothin' on'y the win', and the rain polthoguin', I very well know."

"And are you certain that the bridge hadn't been mended?" said the District-Inspector.

"How could I help bein' sartin sure? And I goin' by it on'y a while before, in the grey of the light, and Mrs Duggan herself bawlin' across to me that they were kilt thrampin' half-a-mile or so afore they could git over anywheres."

"But if you didn't wait, how do you know that he mayn't have turned back?"

"Wait? Bedad no, it's runnin' away down here I was, as fast as I could pelt. But what was to turn him back, and he flourishin' off wid himself in the greatest hurry at all? You might ha' thought it was ten fine fortin's he was goin' after; and not a stim to see a step before him wid. So if it isn't a murdher, get me one. And that's the raison I was thinkin' I'd a right to be mentionin' it to yourself, sir, or the Sargint."

"It's a very curious case," said the District-Inspector, beginning instinctively to grope about for precedents, and finding none.

"But murdher or no," said Hugh, "I do be thinkin' diff'rent ways of it, and some of them's bad. For I sez to meself, 'In a fine disthraction poor Dan 'd ha' been, when he heard tell of th' ould crathur breakin' her heart in the House.' And then again I sez to meself, 'And supposin'? Many's the fine disthraction you've been in yourself, me man, and niver tuk a lep into the river out of it.' And arter that agin sez I to meself, 'But sure, if some one 'd ha' up and shoved me over unbeknownst, so to spake, sorra the blame I 'd ha' blamed him.' However, since the day 's light'nin' overhead, little doubt I 've had in me mind but that I 'd liefer see him comin' along the road on his feet, disthracted or not disthracted ; and that 's what I 'll niver behould, if it was twyste as clear. Terrible clear it is gettin'," he said, glancing furtively up.

The sky was all one floating, drifting greyness, dim and impenetrable even in a place rather low on the east, where many invisible hands seemed to be straining the vast web in devious directions, so that it thinned and paled. But at this moment it rent there right through, leaving a rift filled strangely with a liquid radiance of silver light glowing into amber, which suddenly darted into the eyes of the two men, and threw their shadows across the wet road, and set the puddles on fire.

"Look," said Hugh excitedly, standing up straight and pointing towards the water.

A wave wider and wilder than the others was coming down the river, with something lapt round in it that made a dark core to its turbid brown. But this was borne along no farther than to the first ridged step in the fleeting rapids. There it halted and lay still, while the turmoil of water and foam fell away from about it in a flurry, draining off through the interstices of the boulders, or pouring over their veiled crests. It was the body of a man. One arm hung down against the straight rock-ledge, and the face looked up to the sun-gleam so naturally that when the next wave rushed by, weltering on and on and on interminably over it, the District-Inspector gave a gasp as if something had been taking his own breath.

"There he is, the very way I tould you," said Hugh. At the sound of his voice the District-Inspector turned quickly, and, seeing that he had stepped up on to the low, ivied parapet, made a grasp at him, but was not in time to reach him. "Stop where you are, Dan, one instiant yet," Hugh shouted: "for here I am, too!"

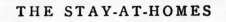

THE STAY-AT-HOMES

THE STAY-AT-HOMES

ON the 1st of March, last year, it might have been noticed that people were continually going in and out of Letterowen Railway Station; yet the number of passengers who arrived and departed by train was certainly no larger than usual. The station is rather a new feature in the village, children of smallish growth remembering a time when its fine pink-washed gables, and brilliant flower-borders, and curious turnstile did not exist; still it had been there long enough for the charm of novelty to have been worn off, and that was not the *comether* which on this dusty-grey, east-windy March Sunday drew thither so many visitors, who had no tickets to buy, nor other official business to transact. What they dropped in to look at was placarded upon the walls of the bare little waiting-rooms, where Jim Neligan, the porter, had been busy with a paste brush the evening before—so excessively so, indeed, being new to his post and zealous, that the station-master had in-quired sarcastically whether he intended to paper the whole place over entirely, and if he didn't think he might as well stick on another layer atop of the first. But the result of Jim's lavishness was that wherever you turned there were the thick black letters announcing a special cheap excursion to Dublin on next Tuesday fortnight, which, as everybody well knew, would be St Patrick's Day. Peter Carroll, who helped to clean lamps at the station, and his mother, who scrubbed floors there, had spread the report of the advertisement overnight, and it sounded so very remarkable that more people than not twirled the turnstile in the course of the morning and came down the zig-zag path to see for themselves.

The inhabitants of Letterowen are not great travellers. Their railway is only a branch of a branch line, and while most of them have not gone farther along it than Brockenbeg Junction, seven miles north, by no means few have never got even so far. It is a place where in soft weather the platform frequently takes a pattern of bare feet, and bare feet seldom set out on long journeys by rail. As for Dublin, that had hitherto seemed a goal which remoteness and magnitude made hardly accessible even to imagination. Letterowen folk considered vaguely that it would need a sight of money and a powerful length of time to bring you thither, and what might be expected to befall you there was so hard to say that your return seemed misty indeed. Yet here was a printed notice boldly promising—"To Dublin and back for two shillings," and going into circumstantial details about a train departing at six in the morning and arriving at noon, and leaving again at midnight. "Twenty-four hours for twenty-four pence," it ended epigrammatically, and some of its readers felt no manner of doubt that each one of them would be an hour of rapture unalloyed. Others were less confident. Old Dan Molloy had heard tell of there being such thick fogs in Dublin most whiles that people "were as apt to walk plump into the river as anywhere else, which was a terrible dangerous thing." And the Widow Loughlin had been told that "thim quare excursion trains as often as not got shunted off into a siding before they came to any place, and the crathurs in them did be left there perishin' for nobody knew how long." Several of the neighbours also wondered whether the people would have to be sitting in their seats all the time she was stopping in Dublin station, for that wouldn't be very gay at all. Mr Farrell, the station-master, was frequently called upon to clear up this or some similar perplexity, and he generally did so satisfactorily, pointing out at the same time that the terms were uncommonly reasonable. I do not think that they struck most of his hearers in just that light. The opinion rather inclined to be that they certainly offered a great deal for the money, but that the money, as certainly, was a great deal to pay. For pence are pennies at Letterowen. Thus the price specified for the four-and-twenty hours had in some cases an effect not intended by the company.

"Four-and-twenty pence—goodness guide us; sure I would be four days arnin' meself that much at the weedin' or stone-gatherin' if I was on full woman's wages itself," said Anne Reilly, who in slack seasons often had to be content with half that amount; "and to go spind it away between one mornin' and the next, as if you could pick it up handy along the side of the road. Musha, long life to them; I hope they'll be gettin' their health till I do."

"And, mind you, the two shillin's isn't the whole of it—where's your bit of food comin' from? Or is it starvin' you'd go there and back again?" said Anne's niece, Katty M'Grehan, meaning to discourage her sister Maggie, whom she suspected of harbouring extravagant ideas, which Maggie quite understood, and rejoined to, saying with some heat: "Then is it aitin' nothin' at all a body'd be, supposin' they was sittin' mopin' at home? 'Twould be all the one thing to take it along in the ould can. For the matter of that there's nothin' aisier."

"Nor wastefuller," Katty said, sticking obdurately to her point, with her worst suspicions confirmed. She wanted to save those two shillings, having planned a treat for her crippled father, "the crathur."

"Well, glory be to goodness, Jimmy," old Mrs Walsh remarked to her contemporary, James M'Evilly, who, like herself, had listened dispassionately to the little skirmish, "you and me is too ould and ancient altogether for to be botherin' about goin' or stayin'—the trees in the hedges is as apt to be thinkin' of takin' runs up the road, and it saves a power of throuble."

This view of the situation prevailed more or less among the elders of Letterowen, but not universally. Here and there an old body held an alert and agile mind, which, according to circumstances, chafed at its restraints, or made a shift to get about in spite of them. Such was the case with Mrs Rea, whose age, never estimated at less than "rale ould entirely," is by some people asserted to be "every day of ninety year." She herself acquiesces cheerfully in any figure between that and threescore and ten. Certain it is, at all events, that she seems quite as active and vigorous as many of her much less venerable neighbours. Still they were surprised when, a few days later, she was amongst the first to announce that she intended to "thry her chance, and see what sort of a place Dublin might be at all at all." Behind her back, they declared that it was "no thing for the ould crathur to take upon herself to be doin'," and that "she might very aisy lose her life over it if she didn't mind what she was at." And some of them called upon her in her house at the end of the post-office row, fronting the railway embankment, for the express purpose of remonstrating with her in scarcely less outspoken terms. "Ah, woman dear," they would say, "is it dotin' you are, or what at all's come over you to put such a notion in your head? Sure it's losin' yourself ten times you'll be going that far, let alone breakin' the ould bones of you clamberin' in and out of them high carriages, and up and down them cruel steep stairs. Or else, ma'am, desthroyed you'll surely be in the streets, where they say an ould person creepin' about is as apt to get dhruv over as a weeny chucken that sets itself up to be runnin' under the people's feet, and they coming out from Mass." But for all of these she had the same answer: "Well now, ma'am, if I amn't ould enough to take care of meself at this time of day, I dunno when I'm likely to be." To which piece of inconsequence they commonly replied, "that them that was wilful'd go their own way," and took leave huffily, unconvincing and unconvinced.

Their axiom was truer in Mrs Rea's case than might have been anticipated from her circumstances; for she was a solitary widow, and the way that such persons go is often determined by quite other considerations than their own wilfulness, especially if there be a question of as much as two shillings involved. Mrs Rea, however, had one son prospering in the States, and another long established as under-gardener to very high-up quality in the county Sligo, and both of them were "rale good lads to their mother," which set her above anything she or her neighbours would have called want. Just now, moreover, her "odd few ould hens," had been laying unusually well, so that her railway fare was forthcoming with little difficulty. The chief obstacle she encountered was public opinion, which, although she thought as lightly of it as might be, she could not completely disregard. It is impossible to set out on a great enterprise with an unperturbed mind in the face of unanimous prophecies that you will never come back alive; even if you do let on to consider them "all blathers and nonsense." So Mrs Rea, while dealing summarily with the objections urged by her ordinary acquaintances, would condescend to argue the matter at much length with her especial crony, Julia Carroll.

Julia disapproved of the project rather decidedly for her, she being by no means an opinionated person. "'Deed, now, Joanna," she said, in the course of their first discussion, "supposin' I had the chance itself, which I havn't, it's long sorry I'd be to be settin' off

on any such a deminted sthravade. Sure,
woman alive, them that has the age on them
of you and me is bound to be travellin'
prisintly, whether or no, far enough to contint
anybody, unless it was the Wanderin' Jew.
So where's the sinse of tatterin' about afore
thin in them racketin' smoky trains? I
declare to you, I hate the noise and smell
of them passin' by there, goodness forgive
me, and it only the nathur of them after
all."

"But bedad thin, Julia, that's the very thing
I was considherin'," said Mrs Rea. "For if
it's stuck down in the one place we're to be
all the while till we're took, we'll get that
disaccustomed to everythin' out of the way
we won't know what to do wid ourselves any-
wheres else. So for that raison we'd a right
to jaunt about now and agin to diff'rint places
the way we'll be a thrifle used to what we're
strange to, and not amazed and moidhered
entirely wid the quareness of it."

"Well, now, I'd never have that notion,"
said Julia Carroll, "for it's the quare quareness and the sthrange sthrangeness I'll be
throublin' me head about when once I get
the chance of goin' the road after some of

them that's wint afore me. Sure as long as there was the ould people in it it might be the most outlandish place one could consaive and I'd niver notice it, I'd be that took up wid meetin' them, nor you wouldn't aither, Joanna. Morebetoken, I'm often thinkin' these times that the old place is the sthrangest of all since they're quit out of it—and no fear of gettin' used to it, sorra a fear!"

"Maybe that's very thrue for you," said Mrs Rea. "But, talkin' of the ould people, there's another raison I have. Do you remimber Biddy Loughlin—thim that lived below the forge?"

"In a manner I remember her, but which of them was Biddy I couldn't say for sure. They was only slips of girls the time they stopped here, and we never had much doin's or dalin's wid them."

"Well, Biddy married a man of the name of Jackson that lives up there in Dublin. Her aunt was telling me she heard from her last Christmas. Keepin' a fine little shop, they are, in some sthreet—I must ask her the name—convenient to the railway station. So I was thinkin' I'd write her word when I was comin', and maybe bid her meet me at the thrain. 'Twould be pleasant to see a body one knew."

"Middlin' pleasant it might be. But, saints above, woman, you needn't tell *me* that you're takin' off up to Dublin for a sight of Biddy Loughlin, that I believe you'd scarce know from her grandmother's ninth cousin, as the sayin' is, if she walked into the room this instiant minyit. For that is too onraisonable a raison altogether."

Mrs Réa looked rather defiantly conscience-stricken. "To spake the moral thruth," she said, "I wouldn't wonder if all the while I wasn't goin' for e'er a thing else except a bit of divarsion; and I dunno if that's any great sin." "Sure not all," Julia Carroll said, more from politeness than conviction, for she was an ascetic both by nature and train-ing. "Only it's the quare divarsion'd take me thravellin' over the counthry if I had a grand little room of me own to be stoppin' paiceable in." She glanced covetously round her friend's house, in which they were talking. For Julia, having lagged superfluously long behind her own generation, was wearing out the fag end of her days in a grand-nephew's family, where the tolerance she met with, though good-natured enough, could not benumb her sense that only in this world she filled up a place which, albeit cold and comfortless, could with difficulty be spared to her. Therefore she looked wistfully round Mrs Rea's domain and said, "Very paiceable I'd stop in it, ay would I."

"There'll be a good few out of this goin' on it besides me, you may dipind," said Mrs Rea, "Dinny Fitzpatrick is, for one, I know."

"Ah, poor Dinny's a young chap, the crathur; where'd he get a ha'porth of wit," said Julia, this time with unintentional severity. "And be the same token, there was his head went by the windy. Gettin' on for six o'clock it must be if he's lavin' work, and I've a right to be steppin' along wid meself."

"Is it wit?" said Mrs Rea; "the lad has plinty of that, according to aught I ever seen of him. If there's anything ails him, it's bein' a thrifle ugly in his temper, as his father was before him. 'Deed, them Fitzpatricks have the name of bein' cross-tempered people— dacint and cross-tempered. That's the way he got quarrellin' wid Norah M'Grehan, she he was spaking to a long while, just about the time she took her situation in Dublin. And my belief is he has some notion now of makin' it up wid her, and that's what's startin' him on the excursion; for until he heard tell of it his mind was set on goin' to the Malahogue Races. I'd be glad if the two of them got frinds ag'in; poor Norah's a good-nathured little girl, the crathur, and all Dinny wants is a bit of humourin' to keep him plisant, and whativer the raison may be, he's mostly seemed as discontinted as an ould hin in a shower of sleet ever since Norah quit."

Denis Fitzpatrick, whose clear-cut profile and rough tweed cap had just crossed Mrs Rea's greenish pane on his way up the dusk-dimmed street, was a good-looking sturdy young fellow, with a countenance which bore out her assertion that he had plenty of wit. She was right, too, in her conjectures about the motive which lay at the bottom of his plans for St Patrick's Day. At that very moment, in fact, he was considering how he might best ascertain Norah M'Grehan's Dublin address without compromising his dignity by any direct inquiries from her family, who had been stiff enough for some months past. He thought he would ask ould Mrs Rea, who was likely to know, and, failing her, Norah's sister Maggie, as she looked several degrees less forbiddingly upon him than Katty had done since the falling out.

But after all he need not have troubled himself with these arrangements. On the afternoon of the Sunday before the holiday Mrs Rea was happily busy over her fire when a long shadow fell in at her door and ran up the wall.

"Well, Dinny," she said, recognising it without turning her head, "and what's the best good news wid you?"

"Och nothin' at all, ma'am," said Dinny.

"There couldn't be less," Mrs Rea said cheerfully; "I'm makin' meself a bit of griddle bread to take along in the thrain, and I'll ha' plinty for you in it too, Dinny."

"Thank'ee kindly, ma'am," Dinny said, gloomily, "but divil a thrain I'll be thravellin' in."

"Mercy on us all—what's after happ'nin' you, man?" she said, whirling round in consternation.

"Sure because I'm claned out—stone broke," said Dinny. "Didn't I put me half-crown on Black Knot, that was runnin' yesterday for the Balmarina Cup, and what'd suit the baste but to go break his ugly neck at the first lep? It was Sargint Duffy himself bid me put every penny I could on him, and he knows people that knows all manner. Two pounds he had on him himself. The divil's in it."

"You great, big, stupid ass, you," said Mrs Rea. "Och, well now, wouldn't anybody think an infant child might have the sinse to keep. out of them ould barracks, where it's bettin' and foolery the len'th of the day? And small blame, maybe, to the polis, that's nothin' betther to do, and plinty of money to be pitchin' under the horses' feet; but for the likes of you to go settin' up to ruinate yourself! Faix but you're the quare fool." Her genuine vexation at his mishap came to the surface in a bubbling of wrath, while her plain speaking was made all the more natural by the fact that it seemed to her only the other day since six-foot Dinny stood scarcely as high as her table, and that in Dinny's recollections Mrs Rea had always been a rather comical old personage, from whom desirable sugar-sticks and cakes and negligable threats and reproaches were occasionally forthcoming. "The grandest chance at all," she said, "and everythin' settled—and Norah, the crathur. Och, now, Dinny Fitzpatrick, if yourself's not the most unchancy stookawn of a gomeral on the townland, just get me him that is?"

"I've raison to be greatly obligated to you, ma'am," said Dinny; "and the next time I want somebody to gab the hind leg off a dog, I know where to be comin' to." So he went away in high indignation. Whereupon Mrs Rea thought ruefully to herself, "Sure, maybe I'd no right to be annoyin' him, and he disappointed wid losin' his holiday and all, the mislucky bosthoon."

Annoyed him she had, however, so seriously, that next evening he had twenty minds at least to make as if he did not hear her calling him across the street, when he was going by from his work. Only that there seemed to be a hoarse sort of despair in her "Dinny, man, Dinny," resentment would undoubtedly have got the better of him; but as it was, he came over and asked what ailed her.

Mrs Rea looked rather dreadful, for she had her head muffled in two large shawls, one grey and one black, and had wisped round her throat a white apron, which gave a curious conventual touch to her appearance. She explained that she was destroyed with a very bad cold, some sort of asthmy or influ-

enzy she thought it must be, it had come on so
sudden, and her corroborative coughs were quite
alarmingly loud. "Ne'er a fut'll I git out to-
morra," she said, "not if the city of Dublin was
just across the width of them two rails there,
instid of len'th-ways. And me writin' word to
poor Biddy Loughlin I was comin' at twelve
o'clock. Lookin' out for me she'll be."

"Sure you could aisy send her a message
be some of them that's goin'," said Dinny.
"Art Walsh is, I know, and his sisther."

"'Deed but I wouldn't like to be disthress-
in' them to be wastin' their day runnin' about
after me messages," Mrs Rea said, "nor I
wouldn't like poor Biddy to be losin' her time
expectin' me."

"Well, thin, I dunno how you can manage
it," said Dinny. "One thing or the other you
must do—send it or let it alone."

"Where's yourself, lad?" said Mrs Rea.

"And didn't I tell you I hadn't a penny
to me name? Not unless it's borryin' I was,
and then where'd me wages be on Sathurday?
I wouldn't mind if it was meself only, but I
can't be lavin' the ould bodies at home too
short, and that's the end of it. There's no
use talkin'."

T

"Och, you gaby, wasn't I manin' you to go on me own couple of shillin's in place of meself, and take me message? Supposin' you 'd nought betther to do. It 's too late to be writin' be the post, and if Biddy doesn't get word, as like as not she 'll be in a fine fantigue, considherin' I 'm lost and sthrayed away; but when you tould her that kilt wid a cowld was all I was, she 'd know nothin' ailed me. Quite convanient she lives to the station, so 'twouldn't delay you above a minyit, and then all the rest of the while you could be seein' anybody else there was, and the sights of Dublin, and everythin'." Mrs Rea was so bent upon recommending her plan that she forgot her hoarseness and bad cough. However, this signified little, as Dinny was too well pleased with the project to be critical about symptoms.

"I give you my word, Judy, woman," she said, when shortly afterwards relating the incident to her friend, "the eyes of him shone out of his head at the notion like the two bright lamps in the tail end of the thrains runnin' by there on a black night."

Thus it came to pass that Denis Fitzpatrick was after all one of the party who on the morrow made an early start from Letterowen. It was a still, soft morning, discreetly hooded in grey, but with an indefinable atmosphere abroad, as if the air were full of some secrets that might be told when the sun got a little higher. Quite a crowd of the neighbours were on the platform seeing the excursionists off, some of them with rather envious eyes. And among those malcontents was Maggie M'Grehan, who felt herself aggrieved by her failure to capture her railway fare, notwithstanding that she had the prospect of a drive to the Malahogue Races for her holiday amusement while her sister Katty looked after their bedridden father. Her mood lightened, however, at the sight of Denis actually starting with the rest, because, for reasons of her own, she had been considerably put out by the stoppage of his expedition.

Mrs Rea did not appear. Of course it would have been unwise of her to venture out with her cold, although her violent cough had wonderfully subsided. But she saw the train whisked by as she was making herself very busy over cleaning up the inmost recesses of her dresser; and her comment was, "Ah, well; sure 'twould ha' been a pity to stand in their way, the crathurs." Her day after this passed without noteworthy incidents until about tea time, when, as she and Julia Carroll were sitting quietly at the brightening fire something unwelcome occurred. To all appearances, it was nothing worse than the entrance of a pleasant-looking, dark-eyed girl, in a becoming velvet-trimmed hat and neat cloth jacket; yet the tone of the ejaculations with which Mrs Rea greeted her clearly betokened an untoward event. "Och, glory be to goodness, is it yourself here, Norah M'Grehan? Whethen now, how did you come whatever? Isn't the childer at your place took sick, the way you couldn't git lave at all, so Katty was tellin' me—the last time you wrote?"

"But sure they've got finely now, and the misthress is takin' them out to Dalkey for a bit of a change. I wrote home word on Sathurday. Didn't they tell you?"

"Deed no; I seen naither of them; and there I am after packing off poor Dinny Fitzpatrick up to Dublin this mornin' arly. Ragin' he is this minyit of time, you may depind, findin' nobody in it."

"And what'd ail him tó be ragin'?" said Norah, "or what call'd he have to be thinkin' of findin' anybody? He knew as well as I did I was comin' down to-day. So off he wint, and joy go wid him and the likes of him. Be good luck I'll be out of it on the eleven o'clock train to-night afore he's back."

"Well, if he knew, it's a quare thing," Mrs Rea began.

"Quarer it'd be if he didn't," Norah said, interrupting, "when he heard it from Maggie last night. Katty was tellin' me— for Maggie's off to the races—she seen her talkin' to him outside, so she was checkin' her for havin' anythin' to say to him, not bein' friendly these times, since he took up- on himself to give me impidence about the Molloy's party. And Maggie said he stopped her to ax would I be comin' home on the holiday, and she tould him as plain as she could spake that I was. So that was the way of it, and the best thing could happen."

"Well, well, well, but that bangs Banagher," Mrs Rea said, not disguising her chagrin. "What was he up to then at all? Troth now, you might as aisy make an offer to count the grains of sugar meltin' in your tay as tell the contrariness and treachery there does be in another body's mind. But we'd betther just be sittin' down; 'twill be drawn be this time. Wait till I reach down a cup and saucer for you, Norah alanna; it's somethin' to git a sight of you at all evints."

It is to be feared that Norah did not find this tea a very lively entertainment, although she talked away at a great rate, telling all her Dublin news. Mrs Rea listened with only a divided attention, the other half, and the largest, being occupied by the thought that after all she might better have gone on the jaunt herself. A sacrifice thrown away is generally an irritating and depressing subject for meditation; and Mrs Rea's seemed to have been worse than merely wasted, as she said to herself that "all the good her stayin' at home had done anybody was only harm." These reflections made her a dull and silent hostess. Then, during a pause in the conversation, Julia Carroll expressed her belief that she herself "as like as not wouldn't be dhrinkin' tay any-wheres by next St Patrick's Day." The little old woman spoke in a hopeful tone, looking as if she saw many pleasant possibilities in the conjecture; but a slip of a girl of Norah's age and experience could scarcely share that view, and the remark did not tend to cheer her.

However, when they had finished tea, Mrs Rea went out into the grey dusk at the door to collect her hens with the few crumbs, and a moment afterwards Norah, who was putting turf on the fire, heard a sound that made her drop the sod out of her hand suddenly enough to set the white ashes fluttering about like snow-flakes, while the golden sparks darted up straight like shooting stars. It was Mrs Rea exclaiming: "Och, mercy be among us! is it yourself, Dinny Fitzpatrick? And what at all brought you back so soon, and how did you conthrive to come?" To which the voice of Dinny replied: "Sure, ma'am, when I got there I found there was nothin' to be keepin' me in it whatsome'er, so one of the guards at the station was a dacint chap from Youghal, and for the sixpence I had along wid me for a dhrink, he let me come back on the two o'clock mail that stops next to nowhere for man or baste, and that way I got home very handy. And was you seein' anythin' to-day of Norah M'Grehan? But, bedad, 'twould be just of a piece wid the rest of it if she was on the road thravellin' back to Dublin agin now."

"Musha, thin, she's not got very far yet, that's sartin. But, goodness help you, man alive, wouldn't it ha' been a dale more sinsible to ha' axed the question afore you took skytin' the len'th of the counthry, and nothin' at the end of it?"

"And, begorra, didn't I ax it? Sure I knew there was some talk of her comin' home, so I axed her sisther Maggie last night, and no, sez she, sorra a fut could she get lave."

"It was an onthruth she tould you," said Mrs Rea.

"Troth, now, I had me doubts it was, ever since the ould woman I seen at her place in Dublin said she well remembered Norah writin' home to say she was goin'; and, if I'm not mistaken, it's not the first ugly turn that Maggie's after doin' agin us. But did you say, ma'am, that Norah was above at her house?"

"What for would *I* go to be tellin' lies on you? Sure, not at all, but if you've a fancy to be standin' on the one flure wid her, just step your feet over the hins' ould dish, and there you are."

Dinny stepped accordingly, and immediately afterwards found himself shaking hands vehemently with Norah M'Grehan, and inquiring what way she was this long while. Norah replied that she must be running home to her

poor father and Katty, for she'd presently have
to be settin' off again to catch the Dublin train.
But Mrs Rea, bustling jubilantly about the
dresser, said, "Aisy now, honey. You'll give
the poor lad time just to swallow his cup of
tay, and then he'll be all ready to go along
wid you."

While Dinny gulped down a very hot
mixture of sugar chiefly and grounds, Julia
Carroll took the opportunity to draw from
the events of the day a moral in support of
her favourite contention against travelling about,
pointing out what a sight of trouble it would
have saved if Dinny had "stopped paiceably
at home, the way he needn't ha' been scaldin'
and chokin' himself for want of a few minutes
to spake to his frinds." Mrs Rea, however,
rejoined—"And supposin' Norah had took it
into her head to stop paiceable where she was
too, where'd the both of them be this evenin'?"
And although she answered readily enough,
"Sure, where Norah was, she wasn't at home,"
the argument did not convince anybody. Certainly not Mrs Rea. For when Dinny had
just started with Norah he wheeled round
suddenly to make a penitent confession. "Och,
murdher! Och, Mrs Rea, ma'am, I niver

remimbered it till this instant, but tellin' you the thruth, I niver went next or nigh the ould woman you bid me be bringin' word you wasn't comin'—cliver and clane I forgot it, and went off straight to look for the Square—Well now, wasn't I the bosthoon?"

"Sure, no matther," Mrs Rea said, blandly. "It's little Biddy Loughlin 'd be troublin' her head about me goin' or stayin', for the thruth is, there was niver much love or likin' between any of us and any of thim."

Dinny looked hard at her for a moment, "And another thing I disremimbered," he said, "was to be axin' you after your terrible bad cowld."

"Bedad, Dinny, I'm thinkin' it wint off to Dublin along wid you," she said. "Anyhow it's quit away surprisin'."

"It's my belief, you're a great ould rogue, ma'am, yourself and your cowld," said Dinny. "But I'd as lief I hadn't lost thim two shillin's and everythin' on you."

"Sure what matther at all?" Mrs Rea said again. "And who can tell but I mightn't get as good a chance next St Patrick's Day, and be travellin' up to Dublin iligant after all? I wouldn't wonder if I was—there's time enough."

A PROUD WOMAN

A PROUD WOMAN

PETER MACKEY, the Carrickcrum
Doctor's man, introduced me to Mrs
Daly one early summer morning, when her
table was flecked with small quivering shadows
by the young beech leaves. That such a
ceremony was required argued me a stranger
to the place, for "ould Anne Daly" at her
stall had a speaking acquaintance with almost
every passer-by. Her rickety deal board
stood at the cross-roads under the beech-
tree whose trunk was built into the wall
behind the National School, where she had a
view of Carrickcrum's street on either hand,
and looked up the road to the bridge, and
down the road to the police barracks as well.
She was a picturesque figure in her black
gown and bluish apron ; for her hair made
white light beneath broad cap frills hooded
with a heavy grey shawl, and the brown eyes
among their weather-worn wrinkles still glanced
as brightly as the waters of a bog-stream.
Her knitting-needles twinkled up at them,
in and out of the dark, rough stocking-leg

that lengthened in her hands, as she sat perched on a crippled chair, dexterously propped against the beech's roots. Upon the planks before her glowed a small heap of half-a-dozen oranges, and as many pink sugar-sticks protruded from a white Delft jam-pot. That was all her stock-in-trade, and even the golden dance over it of the spangling sunbeams could not give it an opulent aspect. What caught my eye at once, however, was a signboard nailed to the trunk just above her head, bearing on a brilliant ultramarine ground, in letters of fiery vermilion, the words :—

The Sentrall Imporeom.

The inscription somehow took my fancy, and I had scarcely beheld it when I seemed to be reading in the catalogue of a certain art exhibition : "No. 34. The Sentrall Imporeom, by Charles Hamilton, price ——." Where-upon followed a vision of the corresponding work—the quaint old country woman pre-siding over her simple wares beneath her leafy canopy and grandiloquent label, with perhaps a hint of the village street in the distance to explain the situation. I presaged "a hit," and felt impatient to set about it at

once. There was a grass-patch over the
way that would conveniently accommodate my
easel. Then I wondered who had put up the
gaudy signboard, and why; whether in pomp-
ous earnest, or intending a jest at the poor
little establishment: and what might be Mrs
Daly's sentiments on the subject. So, with
a design to elicit these, I remarked: "That's
a fine piece of painting you have up there."

"'Deed now is it, sir?" Mrs Daly replied,
darting a quick look at me to ascertain
whether my admiration was unfeigned, much
as I have seen her prove the soundness of
her pears with the point of her knitting-
needle. It stood the test with effron-
tery, and she proceeded: "That was Joe
Lenihan. He done it last winter wid the
bit of paint he had over after finishin' Mr
Conroy's new cart. Joe's a terrible handy
boy. It's got a nice apparence off it, to
my mind, and ne'er a harm at all that I
can see; but, och! the Gaffneys were ragin'
mad over it — them at the shop below
there, sir." She pointed down the street,
and I took a few steps backwards to get a
glimpse of its single plate-glass pane, which
displayed groceries, hardware, millinery, and

other things, and above which ran, large and yellow, "GENERAL EMPORIUM." "Ragin' they were," Mrs Daly said in a tone that was half-gratified and half-rueful. "Sure to this day they won't look the way I am. But I dunno what call they have to set themselves up to be the only Imporum in the place, and they just 'P. Gaffney,' sorra a hap'orth more, and plenty good enough, for them, until before last Christmas they got a man over from Newtownbailey to do their paintin'. There was nobody here aquil to it, I should suppose. So now they're of the opinion I had a right to ha' hindered Joe of doin' me a Imporum as well, and I wid ne'er a notion he was plannin' any such a thing. Howsome'er, he made a very good job of it, sir, as you was sayin'."

"It's a fine morning, Mrs Daly," someone said at my elbow, and, turning round, I saw beside me a tall, respectable-looking young man in a grey tweed suit. "I'm just after shooting old Mr Carbury dead with the rook-rifle, and throwing him over the wall into the river below at Reilly's," he said.

"And is it yourself, Mr Ned? I never heard you comin'. Well now, but you're terrible wicked to go do the like of that,"

Mrs Daly said, as placidly as she had praised Joe Lenihan's handiness. "It's hangin' you they'll be this time for sartin. So you're off to the barracks?"

"Straight," said Mr Ned gravely, "and they needn't offer to say it's manslaughter either, for it's an awful murder. You might have heard the shot. But to see him rolling down the river, over and over—I didn't wait till he sank, for it's time I gave myself up on the charge of committing a cold-blooded murder."

He strode away abruptly with an air of solemn fuss, and Mrs Daly said, looking after him commiseratingly: "He's a son of the Clancys at Glen Farm. Asthray in his mind he is, the crathur, and scarce a mornin' but he comes by here on his way to the polis wid a story of some quare villiny he's after doin'. My belief is he dhrames them in the night, and when he wakes up he can't tell the differ as a sinsible body would. Anyhow he niver harmed man or baste. But sure the Sargint and all of them up there knows the way it is, and they niver throuble their heads about his romancin', or now and again they put him up in the guard-room for a while, just to contint him.

U

"Only one day be chance he landed in on them when there was nobody in it except a young constable that was new to the place, and him he had in a sarious consternation wid the slaughtherin' he was tellin' him of. Fit to raise the counthryside he was before the other men came home. It's as good as a play to hear Joe Lenihan tellin' it. 'Deed now, we'd maybe do betther to not be takin' divarsion out of the crathur's vagaries, that's to be pitied, the dear knows. But sure your heart might be broke waitin' for somethin' to laugh at, if you was to look black at everythin' wid a grain of misfortin in it, for that comes as nathural as the grounds in your cup of tay."

So Mrs Daly philosophised; and when she had finished I bought an orange, and went on my way.

This, however, was only the first of many visits to the Sentrall Imporeum. My wish to paint it and its proprietress continued, and she presently gave me a series of sittings, in the course of which I learned a good deal about her character and affairs. Mrs Daly lived close by, in a very miserable little shanty, windowless and chimneyless, built against a sunken bank, so that its ragged thatch was on a level with the roadway. How she lived seemed less obvious than where, as although she owned three or four hens, and did some coarse knitting while she sat all day at the table with its screed of sweets and fruit, one would have estimated the combined profits of these to fall far short of sufficiency for even her modest wants. Her lameness debarred her from more active industries, she having been crippled by an accident at the same disastrous period—about thirty years before—when her husband died, and her son 'listed, and her daughter married an emigrant to the States.

Perhaps it should be reckoned as another disability that she was the proudest woman in the parish, to whom an offer of assistance seemed an insult, and who would accept nothing from her neighbours beyond a most rigorous equity. For instance, Arthur Kelly, the struggling farmer who owned the shed which she inhabited, would gladly have allowed her to occupy it rent free, but was obliged every week compunctiously to receive sixpence.

I myself experienced the same sort of thing in my trivial dealings with her. Small artifices, prompted by baffled speculations as to how she made out a subsistence, all signally failed. If I contrived one day to over-pay for a purchase, pleading want of change, on the next the undesired pennies were sure to be awaiting me inevitably and inexorably. She refused point-blank to sell me the crushed and over-ripe gooseberries with a fancy for which I had been seized, and she insisted upon taking a farthing apiece off the price of some apples that were fully half-sound. In fact, I was soon compelled to desist from practising any such stratagems, perceiving that our sittings and conversations would otherwise abruptly end. But being wise in time, I kept on good and improving terms with Mrs Daly, and made my studies at the Sentrall Imporeum desultorily all through the summer. Still, when it drew to a close, I was quite aware that our friendliness had not brought me a step nearer venturing upon any attempt to undermine her rigid principle of independence.

This being so, I was not a little surprised when one wet evening at tea-time Mrs Daly paid me a visit for the purpose of asking me to do her a favour. The cottage I had taken that summer stands on the same side of the road as her tiny cabin, but about

half - a - mile farther from Newtownbailey.
It belongs to the brother-in-law of Peter
Mackey, Dr Kennedy's man, which is how
I came to hear of it, and it contains no less
than three rooms on the ground — literally
ground—floor, besides two little attics huddled
up under the thatch. As it has a strip of
privet hedge in front, and a path three flag-
stones long leading to the door, and a hen-
house leaned-to against one end, it may
be considered superior to the neighbouring
residences, though unsophisticated mud and
straw are the main ingredients in its, as well
as in their, composition. With the help of
loans from my friend the Doctor, and some
properties of my own, I had furnished it in
a style which I believe excited admiration
on the whole. Yet the establishment did
not reach the standard of what was deemed
appropriate for "rael quality," especially as I
did for myself single-handed, with only an old
woman from next door to "ready up" things
in the morning; and my social standing was
consequently always regarded as an ambiguous
and perplexing point at Carrickcrum.

Mrs Daly arrived with something evidently
on her mind. She was not likely, indeed, to

have undertaken that slow and painful hobble through the pelting rain without some object; but she seemed to find much difficulty in disclosing it. At last, however, having repeated incredibly often that it was "a very soft night intirely," she made the following more pertinent statement:—

"I'm after gettin' a letter to-day from me brother Hugh's son. That was Hugh went out to the States I couldn't tell you what ould ages ago, and be all accounts he's made the fine fortin in it. But the time he went I was about gettin' married, and he set his face agin that altogether. No opinion he had of poor Andy, that wasn't to say very well to do, and maybe not over-steady. So he wouldn't allow me to be spakin' to Andy at all, and he was wantin' me to go out along wid himself, for Hugh and I were always frinds. Infuriated he was when he couldn't persuade me; the last time I seen him, there was no name bad enough for him to be callin' poor Andy, and he up and tould me that, as sure as he was alive, the next time he set eyes on me 'twould be beggin' he'd find me, unless it was in the workhouse. And sez I to him he might make his mind

aisy that, whativer place he might find me
in, the on'y thing I'd be beggin' of him'd
be to keep himself out of it. And we've
niver been friendly since. Sorra the letter
I've wrote to him, nor he to me. But
now there's the young chap writin' me word
from Queenstown that he's crossed the wather
to see the ould counthry, and that before he
wint his father bid him go look up his Aunt
Nan while he was at home. Sure, I scarce
thought he as much as knew where I was
livin' these times. So me nephew's comin'
to-morra on the train to Newtownbailey. . . .
Well, now, you know me house, sir? It isn't
too bad a little place at all, but you couldn't
say it was very big."

You certainly could not say so, upon almost
any scale of measurement, or with any approximation to truth, I reflected ; for I had seen its
tenant creeping in and out at its low black
doorway, which would hardly have made an
imposing entrance to an average rabbit-burrow.

"And I was thinkin'," she continued, "that
if the young fellow come there, it might be apt
to give him the notion I was livin' in a poorish
sort of way—for the dear knows what quare
big barracks of places he's maybe used to at

home—and I'm no ways wishful he'd bring back any such a story wid him to his father, after the talk he had out of him about the workhouse and the beggin'.

"And another thing is, Hugh'd say 'twas next door to it, me sellin' them hap'orths of sweets outside there; he would, sure enough, for none of me family done the like ever. Och, I'd a dale liefer he'd ha' sted away; but I can't put him off of comin'. And I was thinkin' —I was thinkin', sir . . . ." But Mrs Daly's further thoughts could not be put into words without much stumbling and hesitation. "What I was thinkin' was, that if be any chance you were out paintin' the way you do mostly be, sir, after dinner-time to-morra, you'd be willin', maybe, to let me bring me nephew in here just for the couple of hours he has to stop— comin' on the half-past two train he is, and lavin' on the five—and loan me the fire to make him a cup of me own tay. For then, sir, you see, he could niver say a word to any-body except that I was livin' rael dacint and comfortable—ay, bedad, it is so," she said, glancing wistfully round the ruddily-lighted room. "But it's a terrible dale to be axin' you; and very belike 'twill be a pourin' wet

day, and you not stirrin' out," she added, looking behind her as if she had several minds to
vanish away through the dim rain without
waiting for an answer.

I lost no time in cordially assenting to her
plan, and the sympathy inspired by a sincere
commiseration for her dilemma, caught as she
was between two scathing fires of pride, enabled
me, I believe, to convince her that I really
expected to derive some benefit from the pro-
posed arrangement, as I pointed out how, only
for her presence there, the house would be
left empty all the afternoon, a probable prey
to passing tramps. I mentioned also that, if I
happened to appear upon the scene, it might be
in the character of her lodger. These sugges-
tions seemed to relieve her mind. But as she
was turning to go, a difficulty occurred to me.

"How will your nephew find his way here,
Mrs Daly?" I said. "If he asks it, you know,
they 'll direct him to the wrong place."

"Why, sir," she said, "I was intindin' to
step over wid meself and meet him at the
Newtownbailey station. I 'll get him aisy
enough, for there does mostly be no such
great throng on the platforrm"—(arrivals generally averaged about three) — "that I 'd have

much throuble sortin' him out. And then I could bring him along back wid me as handy as anythin'."

"It's a long walk for you, though," said I, for Newtownbailey is a good two miles from Carrickcrum, and a mile was a mile indeed, at the little old woman's "gait o' goin'."

"Sure I'm well used to it," said she, "I do be thravellin' it these times every Saturday after me few sugar-sticks. At Gaffney's here I was gettin' them for a great while, but ever since I set up the Sentrall Imporum, they're chargin' me fi'pince a dozen, and that I couldn't afford. Ould Gaffney himself he sez to me the laste they could do was to be puttin' on a pinny to the price, now that I'd took to keep such a grand place. But fourpince is all I have to pay at Newtownbailey."

"That was a spiteful trick," I said. And a reply came from without, as the speaker departed over the slippery, wet flags:

"What can you get from a hog but a grunt?" said Mrs Daly.

The morrow was not wet, as she had foreboded, but rather sultry and showery. In the morning, with the help of my friend the Doctor's wife, I made some preparations for my coming guest. Part of these consisted in hanging up on my wall-hooks sundry warm woollen skirts and bodices, and a fine lilac-ribboned cap, with respect to which I cherished designs. Also I spread a table with the materials for a tea, comprising a richly-speckled barn-brack, and a seed-cake pinkly frosted.

I meant to go a-sketching for the day, but had not yet started when, about noon, I saw Mrs Daly toiling up to the door laden with a large basket—come, no doubt, to make final arrangements, before proceeding to fetch her nephew from the station. I was in the little room adjoining the kitchen, and, as the door stood slightly ajar, I could watch her unpack her basket. Evidently she had determined to trespass upon my hospitality only to the extent of house-room, for she produced several sods of turf, besides cups, saucers, and tea-pot (which held a drop of milk), paper wisps of tea and sugar, and half a loaf of bread. These being set on the table, I saw her, to my mortification, remove from it the cakes and other eatables, and stow them away carefully out of sight in a press. I noticed, too, that she laid on the shelf along with them a pair of her knitted socks, which, I conjectured—

rightly, as I afterwards learned — were a present to me and a peace-offering to her pride. I blamed myself for not having foreseen this preliminary visit, and deferred my preparations until a time when she would have no opportunity to cancel them. And at first I thought of lingering behind, and re-arranging the tea-table when she had gone; but upon reflection it seemed more forbearing to leave her to her own devices; so I slipped away unobserved.

The picture of the Sentrall Imporeom still lacked a few finishing touches, which I had, fortunately, resolved to give it in the course of that day; and I was at work down there towards three o'clock, when Mrs Daly drove by on a car, sitting beside a well-dressed, middle-aged man. She wore her fine Sunday shawl, whose ample folds of cream and fawn colour could charitably cover many defects in a body's toilette, and she held up her head with an air of resolute dignity, which grew almost defiant at sight of her residence and business premises. She gave me a stately nod as she passed, turning then to her companion with some remark which was, I fancied, explanatory and apologetic. I watched them round the corner, regretting that they were on their way

to such frugal fare, and hoping that the entertainment might go off satisfactorily, despite Mrs
Daly's refusal of my contributions to its success.

The afternoon slid by rapidly on the rollers
of my work, which was interrupted by the
occurrence of more than one sharp thundery
shower. I was still struggling to catch the
effect of a sunbeam blinking Turneresquely on
a little pile of shrivelled oranges, and snatched
away capriciously by shifting clouds, when the
car re-appeared, trotting back very fast with
the same load as before.

"Sure, me nephew," Mrs Daly told me afterwards, "found himself so comfortable up above
there, and was in such an admiration of the
grand little room, that he sted talkin' of all
manner till he'd left himself scarce betther than
a short quarther of an hour to git his thrain, so
he bid the man dhrive for every cent he was
worth. He's a queer, outlandish way of spakin'.
And I sez to him I had some shoppin' to do
in the village, so he was givin' me a lift."

Just as the car passed between my easel and
the beech, a fierce flicker of lightning quivered
through the boughs, causing the horse to shy
with a wide-sweeping swerve, which brought
the car-wheel full tilt against the rickety table,

whose flimsy boards fell asunder, strewing their burdens around, while the sudden jerk flung the old woman on the road.

For a moment I feared some damage more tragical than that sustained by the ruined stall; but Mrs Daly picked herself up with great promptitude, and without any apparent injury. Her presence of mind was evidently unscathed, for she at once remarked, calmly surveying the wreck—

"Bedad, now, that'll be a loss to whatever poor body owns it."

"I expect it will, indeed," said her nephew, who looked much more perturbed than she. "It's considerable of a smash, anyway. But look here, Aunt Anne, perhaps you'd have no objection to taking charge of the dollars to make all square? Because, if you're really none the worse for your fall, I must be making tracks for the depôt, or I'll not get on the cars this evening at all; and I wouldn't miss them for a long figure, and that's a fact."

He was pulling out a bank-note, but his aunt waved it away superbly.

"Ah, no, lad; not be any manner of manes," she said. "Sure, what matter about it? They were on'y a thrash of ould sticks."

"Speak for yourself, Mrs Daly," I said. "The person they belong to wouldn't thank you."

"That's so, sir," said the stranger, who was obviously divided between anxiety to do justice and to avoid delay. "I wonder now would *you* have the goodness to pass this on to the proper party?"

I assented to the proposal with an alacrity which, had it not been for his own hurry, might have struck him as suspicious; whereupon he handed me the note, and drove away. He had placed, I was gratified to learn, ten pounds' worth of confidence in me at first sight.

Long and elaborate, however, were the arguments which I had to use before Mrs Daly would permit me to execute his commission. They were tedious to recapitulate, and the most effective of them was probably the least logical— that, namely, which urged the exultation to be presumed in the mean Gaffneys at her unretrieved disaster. Her scruples yielded to a judicious insistence upon this, and she suffered the making of her fortune. For her acquisition of ten pounds was nothing less than that, as will be readily understood by anyone who has tried to live, for any length of time, on the profits arising from the sale of a dozen half-penny sugar-sticks. It enabled her to rent a much superior dwelling with a window, and to invest in quite a large assortment of miscellaneous goods for exhibition behind the panes, besides adding to her stock of "chuckens"; and, according to latest reports, she was doing grandly. But the Sentrall Imporeom no longer exists. A few days after the accident, the gaudy blue-and-red board was found to have been removed from the beech-trunk—a deed with which the parodied Gaffneys were credited, and at which Mrs Daly felt rather aggrieved, as she had wished to set it over her new door, having given up the hardships of an open-air stall. However, she has plenty of things to pride herself on these times. And, as she moralised: "It's the quare low-lived tricks people does be at by way of settin' themselves up."

THE END